Scholastic Children's Books,
Euston House, 24 Eversholt Street,
London, NW1 1DB, UK

A division of Scholastic Ltd
London ~ New York ~ Toronto ~ Sydney ~ Auckland
Mexico City ~ New Delhi ~ Hong Kong

Published in the UK by Scholastic Ltd, 2008

ISBN 978 1407 10333 4

Printed and bound by Bookmarque Ltd, Croydon, Surrey

2 4 6 8 10 9 7 5 3 1

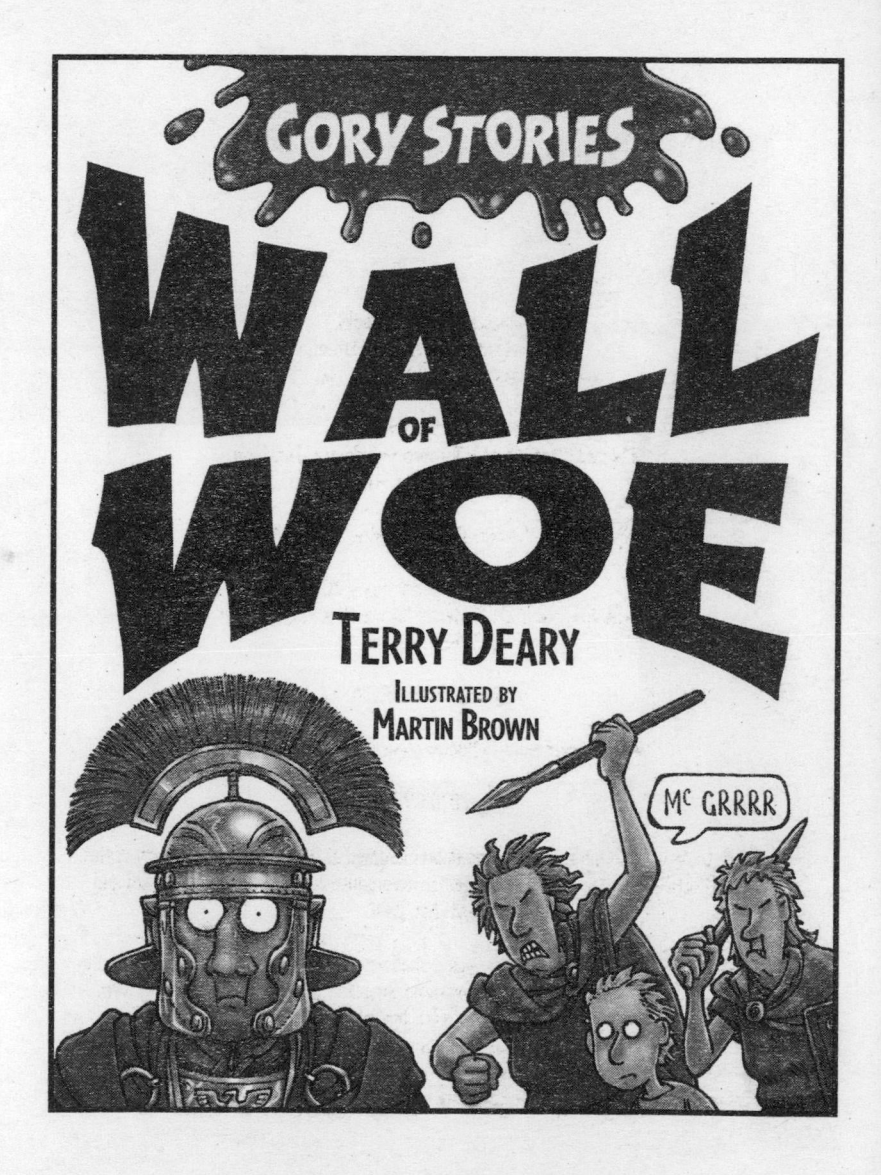

INTRODUCTION

Oh, they were rotten those Romans. Rotten and ruthless. Rotless, in fact.

Their soldiers swept over the north of the world like a plague of pasta. They swarmed over every country they came across and ruled it with a rod of spaghetti.

Then they did something very clever. They made the defeated people do their fighting and conquering for them.

> This is a bit like your school bully thumping you until you agree to thump the other kids in the schoolyard. Then he sits back and enjoys all the stuff you nick for him. So the Romans stayed in sunny Rome and sent other people to fight in the cold, wet north. Good idea? Or rotless?

When the Roman Army reached Britannia it trampled all over the bit we call England. When they reached the country we now call Scotland they stopped.

Maybe they didn't like the terrible tribes they met … the Picts (who were from Scotland) and the Scots (who were from Ireland).

Maybe they just didn't like Scotland – a wild wasteland of big hills, rain, bigger hills, cold winter winds, more rain … and unwashed warriors. Maybe Emperor Hadrian hated the hairy bagpipe-blowers.

So he built a whacking great wall – Hadrian's Wall ... well, HE didn't build it and the people of Rome didn't build it. Those soldiers from the defeated tribes in Europe built it for him.

It worked for a little while ... but in the end the Scots got to England and fifteen hundred years later they were ruling it! (That's the Slimy Stuart family in case you were wondering.)

The Roman Army brought a few Rotless Roman customs with them – sacrificing animals to their gods.

The Romans were even nasty to one another. The soldiers were stuck in the army for 25 years and told they'd get a nice piece of land when they retired ... if they weren't killed first. They weren't allowed to marry so it could get a bit lonely up on Hadrian's Wall.

And cold. Imagine what it would be like if you were a

man from North Africa, or sunny Spain, sent to face the wicked Pictish winds. You're cold and miserable, thousands of miles from home. You're afraid that some powerful Pict might polish you off one moonless night. And if you so much as fall asleep when you are on guard then your own friends will be told to stone you to death. Stone me. What a life!

Imagine it … except you don't have to imagine it. Let me imagine it for you. Let me tell you the tale of some sad souls who wandered the Wall seventeen hundred years ago. Here's the story of Milecastle 13 and the grim Gaul soldiers who worked on the wild Wall…

GUARDS, GRAVES AND GRIME

Arturo and Walachia were Gauls. They were from a place they called Teutoburger ... though you would call it Germany.

Arturo was a handsome young man with flowing, gold hair bristling from the sides of his Roman helmet. His arm muscles strained the seams of his tunic. As he arrived at Milecastle 13 he was sandal-sore and hungry. His handsome mouth was turned down in a scowl. 'I'm hungry, Walli,' he muttered.

The thin, dark soldier beside him said, 'I'm cold.'
A north-westerly wind blew down from Pictland. If it hadn't been made of stone, the Wall itself may have shivered. The nails on the soles of the soldiers' sandals clattered over the cobbles on top of the Wall.

Each milecastle had two towers – one on each side of the gates. The soldiers reached the first tower and entered the door into the top room – the room where they would shelter and sleep. It smelled of dead sheep.

That's because there were fleeces of sheep on the floor for them to lie on. The sheep were dead when they were skinned, which is why the room smelled of dead sheep. See? There is an answer for everything if you know where to look for it.

They threw down their bags and weapons wearily. Suddenly a small, olive-skinned man marched in through the door. From the studs on his sandals to the huge crest on his helmet Obnoctius was no taller than a ten year-old child. But his eyes glowed like oil lamps. Fierce, and just a little wild. His body was small but Obnoctius's voice was large. He pointed at the jumble of bags, weapons and blankets.

'That is no way for a Roman soldier to treat his kit!' he roared.

'We're not Roman ... we're Gaul,' Arturo sighed.

'You have the honour of being in the Roman Army so you will act like a Roman. I of course was born a Roman ... but you are the next best thing. So line up for inspection.'

'It's hard to line up when there are just two of us, Obnoctius,' Walli said with his simple, but charming grin.

The officer glared at him. 'Don't argue, I say, don't argue. You two wastrels are in enough trouble. You are already sentenced to death, remember. One wrong word and I will slice off your insolent heads here and now.'

'Which word?' Walli asked.

'Which word what?'

'Which is the wrong word that will get us the chop?' he asked.

'Upset me and you are dead men.' Obnoctius spluttered. He jabbed a finger at skinny Walli. 'You fell asleep on guard duty … the greatest crime any Roman soldier can commit. The punishment is to be stoned to death by the rest of your troop … the men that you let down.'

'It was a quiet night,' Walli said wearily. 'There was no danger, sir.'

'No!' Obnoctius screeched. 'And why was there no danger? Because I … Captain Obnoctius, led our top troops into Pictland, captured the men of the McKilt tribe and packed them off to Spain to fight for Rome. I have made Hadrian's Wall safe. I … the awesome Obnoctius! One day I will be a general. One day I will win a crown of oak leaves from Emperor Hadrian himself! One day I will return to Rome and they will cheer me to the tops of the temples!'

Arturo gave a wide and loud yawn. Obnoctius turned on him furiously. 'As for you, you great, greedy Gaul…'

'I thought I was a Roman,' Arturo muttered.

'Don't argue … as for you … you ran away in a battle … the greatest crime any Roman soldier can commit.'

Walli opened his mouth to argue but decided he'd be stoned.

'It was a practice-battle – the Gauls against the Nubians. And it started raining,' Arturo said.

'Raining!' Obnoctius screamed. 'Raining! The Roman Empire stretches from the deserts of Africa to the jungles of India. We fight in rain, baking heat and blizzards. We don't let rain stop us!'

'But I'd lost my helmet,' the tall Gaul said with a sigh.

'So what?'

'I was worried I'd get my hair wet … I'd just had it cut and I was going out that night so I…'

'Shut up!' Obnoctius screeched so loud his cheeks were the colour of robins' breasts. 'Stoned! Both of you. A disgrace. There is only one thing between you and a hail of stones.'

'I hope it's a big shield,' Walli said.

'It is ME, you buffoon. Me! I saved you. I saved you because I sent you to Milecastle 13.' He lowered his voice, his eyes bulged like a mad bull, and his breath was short – almost as short as his legs. 'This is a suicide mission, you see? You will probably die here like the others before you! Die, do you hear?' Obnoctius panted and lowered his voice still further. 'The last troop to guard the Wall at this Milecastle vanished last week. Vanished with no trace.'

'The Picts,' Arturo added.

'There are no Picts. The Pict men were all captured in my raid. The Pict tribe has just women and children, I tell you.'

Arturo raised a finger in the air and cut in, 'I read a book by the historian Tacitus. He told the story of British Queen Boudica. She said that the people in these islands are used to being ruled by women. The Pict Queen over the wall, Maggie McKilt, could have defeated the lost troop. Chopped them into pieces and thrown them in the Pictish swamps to be swallowed.'

'Pah!' the Captain spat and waved a hand. 'Boudica! Ten thousand Romans defeated her British army of a hundred thousand.'

'Aha!' the tall Gaul said, raising that annoying finger

again. 'But she had already massacred seventy thousand Romans. The River Thames turned red with blood. As the tide went out the sands took on the shape of corpses.'

'Nasty,' Walli muttered. 'She sounds scary.'

'She is dead … been dead for over a hundred years, I tell you! The seventy thousand she killed were Roman women, children and old men … she took poison once the real Roman Army beat her. And you are not fighting Boudica. You are facing a bunch of women and children led by Queen Maggie McKilt. And on this side of the Wall, if you need help, you have the Britons led by Queen Virago.' The little Roman puffed out his chest. 'Not that you should need the help of our friends the Britons. We are Romans.'

'I'm Gaul,' Walli said.

'I'm hungry,' Arturo added.

'You are dead if you do not succeed. You have two tasks … that is all. First, find out what happened to my missing men – the lost troop. And the second task is simpler – just make sure there is peace between the Picts and the Britons. Keep them apart. If you fail I will tie you to a post and have you stoned.'

'Can I wear my armour?' Walli asked.

The little Captain ignored him. 'I will throw the first stone myself.'

'In Gaul we let a dying man have one last wish,' Arturo said and ran his fingers through his flowing hair.

'And what good would that do you?' Obnoctius sneered.

'I would wish … to die of old age,' Arturo said.

Obnoctius turned an even brighter shade of red. 'Find the lost legion. Keep the peace … or die. Understand?' he said jabbing a stumpy finger into Arturo's armour.

Arturo and Walli nodded glumly.

COBBLES, CATAPULTS AND CRUELTY

'We need help!' Arturo wailed.

The Captain reached up and grabbed the Gaul by the ear. He led him out of the tower and on to the cobbles that ran on the road along the top of the Wall. Then he pulled the ear till Arturo's helmet clattered against the stone parapet. 'You – have – help!' he shouted and with each word he smashed the Gaul's head onto the stones. 'You have a dirty great wall. A wall that is almost as thick as Walli's head. That is your help. I say, THAT is your help. You will keep the peace or die trying.' He tugged at Arturo's ear again and pointed down the road that ran level with the Wall on the British side. 'And look.'

Arturo looked back towards the distant fort. A team of soldiers and ponies were dragging a huge wooden machine along. The men were sweating even in the cruel Pictish wind.

'Yes, sir,' Arturo groaned. 'Can you let go of my ear now?'

Obnoctius ignored him. 'A new catapult. We built it specially for you, Arturo. If the Picts make trouble then load it with boulders and fire them over the Wall. Aim for the Pict village over the hill. That will keep them in their place.' Finally the little Roman let go of Arturo's ear.

Arturo rubbed it and sniffed back a tear. 'Yes, sir.'

'Now guard the Wall with your miserable, worthless lives. There are two of you. One on guard at all times while the other one rests.'

Walli poked his head round the milecastle door. 'Can I be the one that rests?' he asked.

'You take it in turns, you buffoon!' Obnoctius exploded.

'I will check on you when I have the time. I am a busy man, I say, a busy man.'

He turned on the heel of his sandal and began to march away. He made a funnel of his fingers and pretended he was holding a trumpet. As he marched he blew himself a marching song. 'Par-parp-a-parp-parp! Par-parp-a-parp-parp!'

'Captain!' Walli cried after him.

'Par-parp-a-parp-what?'

'You said we had TWO tasks. What were they again?'

'Solve the mystery of the disappearing troop,' Obnoctius called back. 'Keep the peace AND find out what happened to ten good soldiers ... then I may – just MAY – spare you the stoning.'

He turned and marched along the top of the wall and back to the fort over the hill. 'Par-parp-a-parp-parp! Par-parp-a-parp-parp!'

'I'm hungry,' Arturo huffed.

'I'm cold,' Walli shivered.

They slouched over to the Wall and looked up at the ragged clouds that scudded across the cold sky. But they should have looked down. They would have noticed human shapes moving over the moors to the north of the wall. The Picts were watching.

***

Queen Maggie McKilt wriggled over the grass on her large belly. A weedy boy wriggled beside her. He had dark red hair just like hers and he had her pale blue eyes too.

When I say he had her eyes I don't mean he had her eyes. That would be very messy. I mean he had the same coloured eyes. It's a little clue to who he was. Got it?

The four eyes followed Obnoctius along the wall.

The boy groped in the rough, reedy grass for a pebble. He took a leather string from a pocket in his dark woollen kilt. 'Shall I hit him with a stone from my sling, Ma?' he asked.

'No, Don!' she said sharply. 'See that crest on his helmet?'

'Yes, Ma.'

'He's an officer. Maybe a real Roman. If we upset him we'll have the whole Roman Army after us. He's probably the one that ordered the legion to invade last year – and packed your poor Pa off to Rome ... or somewhere just as horrible.'

'Is it horrible in Rome then?'

'Very hot,' the Pict Queen said.

Don McKilt sighed and shivered. 'Sounds nice.'

'There's nothing wrong with Pictland,' she said and smacked her son around the ear. 'It's lovely here – in the summer.'

'Trouble is it's hardly ever summer,' he muttered to himself. He looked up at the dark clouds that raced across the sky and promised rain. The ground they were on would soon turn to a swamp when rain came. He wished he was back in the village over the hill, in the turf hut with the fire of peat glowing hot.

'A fire of peat' is hot and glowing. In the bad old days the Romans reckoned the British druids burned men alive. That is making 'a fire of Pete' and is not the same thing at all.

18

'Can we go home now, Ma?'

'Aye. We'll tell the clan what we've seen,' she said. 'The Romans have sent just two men to guard the milecastle this time. One will sleep while the other stands guard. But there's only a quarter moon tonight and lots of cloud. The one on guard won't be able to see a thing. We'll cross the Wall and back without them knowing.'

'Do we have to cross the Wall, Ma? What if we get caught?'

'Well, son, the Romans like to crucify people – build huge crosses and tie you to them by the hands and feet till you're dead. And when they get bored with that they have a bit of fun throwing you into an arena with some wild animals ... hungry wild animals that want to tear you apart and eat you. Or maybe they'll make you fight with a gladiator – let you battle a wee while before he stabs you to death.' She lay on her back and looked up at the clouds. She smiled a grim smile. 'Oh, the Romans know more ways to kill a lad like you than anyone else in the world. They like to make killing fun.'

'It wouldn't be fun for me if I got caught!' Don wailed. She rolled back on to her belly and smacked him round the head again. 'So don't get caught, Don. Don't get caught!'

'No, Ma,' he sighed.

'Get it into your thick skull,' she said slapping the top of his head till it stung. 'The Ro-mans are cru-el!'

'They're not the only ones,' Don cried, and scuttled back to the McKilt clan village over the hill.

Back in the village a couple of boys had a bundle of heather about the size of a man's head. They were the McGargle brothers and they were throwing it backwards and forwards.

'Want to play, Don?' one of the boys asked.

'Looks boring,' Don said.

'What would you do with it then?' Big McGargle asked.

'I'd do something a bit harder than that – something that needs a bit of skill.'

'Such as?' Little McGargle asked and threw the heather ball to Don. The Queen's son thought. Then he threw it in the air and aimed a kick at it. The ball soared in the air, landed on a roof of reeds and stuck there. Not even the Pictish wind could shift it.

'Aw!' Big McGargle groaned. 'You've lost us our ball!'

'You could climb up and get it,' Don told him.

'No. THAT is Jinny McGargle's roof … our granny! She'd skin us alive and turn our skins into balls if she caught us.'

Don nodded. 'That's the answer,' he told the boys. 'We need an animal skin or a bladder or something to make a proper ball. Then we can play the new game I'm inventing.'

'Ball-kicking?' Little McGargle asked.

'Yes … but I'm going to call it ball-foot and I'm going to be the best ball-footer in Pictland. When I am really brilliant I'm going to challenge the Britons to a game and beat them into the ground!'

'You want to be a foot-ball star?' Big McGargle snorted.

'A ball-foot star,' Don corrected him.

'But you can't be a ball-foot star till you have a ball.'

'All we need is a cow,' Don said.

'A cow? Cows can't play foot-ball!' Little McGargle giggled.

'The game's called ball-foot ... and the cow will be the ball.'

'Uh!' Big McGargle gasped. 'It's a bit big. You couldn't kick that on to Granny McGargle's roof!'

Don shook his head. 'No, I mean we use the cow to make a ball.'

'Cow meat's nice,' Little McGargle groaned. 'I could eat a whole leg to myself.'

'Yes,' Don nodded. 'Let's kill a cow, have a feast on the meat and make a ball from the rest.'

Big McGargle scoffed, 'Brilliant idea, McKilt ... one problem. There aren't any cows on this side of the Wall – not for miles. Cows don't grow on trees, you know.'

'Don't they?' Little McGargle said. 'I thought they did! So where do they grow, big bruv?'

'Shut up, little bruv. The point is our mate McKilt's great plan won't work without a cow.'

'I suppose not.'

Don McKilt grinned a gap-toothed grin. 'But I know where we can get one. And we'll be the heroes of the village when we give the tribe the feast of their lives.'

'We would be heroes!' Big McGargle agreed. 'They get to eat ... we get to play football.'

'How many times do I have to tell you, McGargle ... it's ball-foot. Ball-foot.'

'I think foot-ball sounds better,' the big Pict boy argued and that started a wrestling-punching match that went on till dark.

There are some people who will argue that this is NOT how football was invented. These boring people are called 'historians'. But if you ask them to explain how football came about they will sniff and say, 'We don't know, actually.' So we don't know the game WASN'T invented by a bunch of lads on the borders of Scotland, do we?

RAIN, ROPES AND RAIDERS

If you'd been on guard duty instead of Walli and Arturo you'd have been watching much more carefully, wouldn't you? You'd definitely have seen the red-haired boy half-running, half-crawling back to the hill with his mother. From your place over the tower door you would have seen the tops of the Pict village huts with their peat-smoke rising through holes in the middle of the pointed roofs.

Arturo and Walli could have seen them if they'd climbed to the top of the tower and looked north. But they were busy greeting the troops that had brought the new catapult.

The troops unfastened the ropes that had been used to drag the machine from the fort. A mound of earth ran level with the Wall, about sixty metres south of it. It was a sort of barrier to keep the Britons away from the Wall. A few women and children from the British village stood on the mound to gape at the catapult.

A small woman with wild black hair and a face as fierce as a wolf stood perfectly still and watched. The wind blew her hair into a streaming, whipping, flapping flag behind her. A girl held on to her belt.

The two saw Arturo and Walli trot down the steps from the top of the tower to greet the Romans. And Arturo saw the woman.

'Who is that?' he asked the centurion in charge of the troop. The new men had arrived a few days ago at the fort three kilometres away to replace the missing men. They were from sunny Spain so the cold rain was a pain.

Again and again the men of Spain moaned at the rain and the cold (but the rain in the main) but they argued in vain and it drove them insane (in the brain) as it ran down the drain. (Try saying that with a mouthful of mushrooms.)

'Virago – Queen of the British tribe,' the Spanish centurion replied abruptly. He turned away and bawled at the soldiers. 'Hurry along, lads. You want to get back to the fort before darkness, don't you?'

'Yes, sir!' the soldiers said and fumbled with the ropes in their panic.

'Why the hurry?' Walli asked.

'Because we don't want to be caught in the open after dark, of course, you Gaul goon!' the man said as sweat trickled down from under his helmet.

'Why not?'

'Because we've heard the stories of the Attacotti...'

'The attacking what-i?'

'The Attacotti! The Pict tribe that lives north of the Wall. Don't you know anything? Why do you think you were sent here to guard Milecastle 13?' the centurion asked hoarsely.

'Because we're the bravest of the brave?' Arturo told him.

'No, because you're the useless-est of the useless! The Romans won't mind too much if the Attacotti eat you.'

'Eat us?' Arturo said looking at Walli. 'Why would they want to do that?'

'Because that's what Attacotti like to do!' the officer from the fort explained and began to back away towards the road that led back to the safety of the fort. 'They're cannibals. They say they like human flesh better than sheep or oxen. The lads reckon that's what happened to the lost legion!'

'Eaten?'

'Scoffed by the Picts and Scots. Keep a good lookout or else...'

'Or else?'

'Or else they'll kill you and breakfast on your brains.' Suddenly the Spaniard gave a giggle. 'Not much of a meal in your case. Goodbye!'

He ran after his troop and they vanished into the distance. Back to the safety of the fort three kilometres away.

Arturo looked across to the British Queen standing on top of the Vallum.

Yes, 'vallum' is an awful Roman word. Try to picture two banks of earth with a ditch between – this is the vallum that ran all the way along the Wall on the south side – to keep the Britons away from the Wall ... probably.

'If the Attacotti come will your people help us?'

The woman sneered. 'Don't believe the tales the Romans tell. I've lived here all my life and never seen them eat a soldier ... yet. It's just a story made to frighten fools like you. Cowards.'

This was true. Tales of Attacotti cannibals were never proved. They were probably just stories made up to scare the soldiers into being careful. If YOU knew a man-eating monster was coming to get you then YOU'D stay awake ... wouldn't you?

She turned and began to walk back towards the village in the valley. 'But you'll help us if we call? If they attack?' Arturo called after her.

The girl at the Queen's side turned and cried at them, 'YOU are supposed to protect US, you Roman donkeys.'

'We're Gauls,' Walli said.

'Whatever you call yourselves. In the old days there was a troop of ten men or more in every milecastle. Now there is just a pathetic pair like you!' she snapped.

Arturo spread his hands. 'The Emperor is calling troops back to Rome to defend the city. The barbarians are on the move. They want to destroy the Empire. We're better than nothing!' he insisted.

'We'll see about that,' the girl snorted.

'Dandelion,' the Queen said tiredly. 'Let's fetch the cow for milking and start preparing food for Adrian's visit. He's a great man and we have to show him respect, girl. Let's give him a feast he'll never forget.'

'Yes, Mother.' The girl sighed and rubbed her empty stomach. 'Have you ever had a feast you've never forgotten?'

'Oh, yes,' Queen Virago said smiling.

'When was that?'

'I've forgotten.'

The two walked towards the field where the thin cow was munching even thinner grass.

'Does a queen do her own milking?' Walli asked.

'She does when she's a British queen and you Romans have taken our men away,' she said angrily and marched away, with her daughter Dandelion running to keep up with her.

Arturo shook his head. 'We're on our own, Walli,' he said. The clouds were turning blacker and bubbling up like froth at a mad dog's mouth. A storm was rushing towards them as the sun was setting to the west and painting the distant mountains blood red.

The soldiers ran up the steps to the tower of the milecastle as the first large drops of rain stung their faces.

Arturo tore open his ration bag and looked inside. There were strips of dried meat, a small cheese, some very dry bread and a leather bottle of wine. He started tearing and chewing at the meat and turning it soft with large gulps of the sour wine. 'Ynnnng ynnng nng yngggg nng ynnnng!' he said and showered his partner with half-chewed food.

'What?' Walli asked.

'I said ... you go on guard duty first.'

'What will you be doing?' Walli asked.

'Sleeping,' Arturo told him. 'Don't worry, I'll take your place and let you have a rest.'

'When?'

'Tomorrow morning,' Arturo promised.

'Tomorrow morning!' Walli cried. 'I could be dead by tomorrow morning. I could wake up a skeleton, stripped of all my flesh!'

'No you couldn't – because you're not going to sleep – you're on guard,' Arturo said smoothly. 'If you hear anything unusual just call for me and I'll come and help you.'

'Why don't YOU do night duty first?' Walli asked.

'Hah!' Arturo cried. 'How on earth could I do it? It's raining, you blockhead. I'd get my hair wet!'

'Ah, yes, sorry, I forgot,' Walli muttered.

The rain beat on the wooden roof and Walli shivered in the doorway. 'I can't see a thing out there. It's just too dark.'

'But if they try to break down the gates you'll hear them,' Arturo said. 'In fact my bed here is right over the gates. 'I'll hear them too!'

'Ah!' Walli cried. 'So I may as well stay here in the tower. I'll keep dry but I'll be listening for a Pict attack.'

'Your choice.' Arturo shrugged. 'But if you're staying in just shut the door to this room and keep out the cold.' Walli looked pleased. Arturo rubbed two flint stones together and made enough sparks to light the oil lamp. Walli huddled in his blanket on the sheep-fleece bed and settled down for the night.

Then he did what he usually did on guard duty ... he fell asleep.

***

Don McKilt didn't sleep. When darkness fell he left the warmth of the Pict village and looked towards Milecastle 13. An oil lamp glowed in one of the tower windows.

The Wall loomed grey and gloomy. He peered into the darkness looking for some glint of Roman helmet or armour. Nothing.

He turned to the two boys behind him. 'I can't see anyone on guard. They're not expecting us. So we go ahead with the plan.'

The boys nodded and wrapped their dark woollen cloaks around them and pulled the corners over their heads. They were invisible in the blackness.

So, how did the boys find their way to the Wall, you ask? Some people say the Wall was painted white. So even on the darkest night you could see it glowing like a ghost of a wall ... not that walls usually become ghosts when they die. But if they did, that's what the Wall would have looked like that night.

Rain lashed their bare legs and the ground was turning soft and boggy under their feet. They reached the gate of the Milecastle and pushed at it.

It rattled but wouldn't open. 'Barred,' Don McKilt whispered.

'Will you climb over since there's no guard there?' one of the boys asked.

'No – there's a toilet house on the British side. One of the men in the tower might just come out for a pee and catch me as I reach the top. We'll stick with the plan. I'll go along for a hundred paces, climb the Wall and drop down the other side. I'll come back and open the gate from the British side.'

He was gone as silently as the owl's wing. When he was a safe distance from the tower he threw a rope with an iron hook on the end and it clattered against the top of the Wall before it bit into the stone. Don McKilt was on top in a flash. He rolled up the rope and threw it over his shoulder, then hurried back to the Milecastle. He ran down the steps on the British side and stood for a moment. There was no sound other than the moaning wind and the beating of rain in the puddles on the ground.

He slipped into the darkest shadow of all – the passage between the towers. In the blackness he fumbled for the wooden bar. It was heavy and he was a small boy but his wiry arms pushed it upwards. The bar was swollen with the damp and had stuck.

He pushed with all his strength and the bar came loose suddenly. It flew up and out, then fell on to the cobbles. The wooden gates were blown open by the northern wind and smashed against the walls of the towers.

The two Pict boys didn't have time to worry about the noise as they hurried through and helped Don close the gates and drop the bar back in place. They sped south, over the road, over the mound of the vallum and hid in its shelter, panting.

They looked back over the mound and waited for guards to come rushing out, blowing trumpets to call for help.

'We're trapped if the troops arrive. We're on the wrong side of the Wall,' one of the boys moaned. 'You were supposed to open the gates quietly, Don! You said we have to be quiet.'

Don grabbed him by the front of his cloak and said, 'Then try not to cry too loud when I smash your teeth down your throat, McGargle!'

'Sorry, Don. Sorry!' the boy squeaked. The boys lay on the wet grass of the mound and looked back towards the Milecastle. There was no sound and no movement.

Inside the tower Walli the Gaul had jumped when the bar clattered to the ground and the gates crashed open.

'What was that?'

'Go and see,' Arturo suggested.

'Come with me?'

'No, I'm asleep. You're the one on guard duty.'

Walli opened the tower door and the rain slapped his face. He leaned over the parapet and looked down at the gate. It was closed … well, it would be. The Pict boys had moved quickly – Walli hadn't.

The guard hurried back into the shelter of the tower room. 'The gates are shut,' he reported.

'That's all right then. It was probably just a branch blown up against the gates. You'd be scared of your own shadow!' Arturo laughed. 'Now be quiet and let me get some sleep.'

The tall Gaul wrapped himself tight in his blanket and turned his back on Walli.

Walli sat with his back against the Wall and listened. Owls hooted but their haunting cries were swept away by the wind. The gates rattled but didn't crash open again. The gusts made them shake then stop, shake then stop, shake then stop. Walli closed his tired eyes.

The next thing he heard was a voice saying, 'What's for breakfast?'

'Uh?' he mumbled, rubbing his eyes. 'Breakfast? Are the Attacotti going to eat us for breakfast?'

'No! What are WE going to eat for breakfast? It's morning,' Arturo said.

Walli had slept through his guard duty.

And that, as you know, was nothing new.

But the last time he did, it didn't matter. This time was different…

34

MUSIC, MUD
AND MEAT

Dandelion's feet made no sound as they flew up the steps to the top of the milecastle tower. But her stony fists made a huge sound as they pounded on the door. 'Come out you, Roman clowns! Come out so my Ma can kill you!'

Walli blinked and tried to back away to the farthest wall. But he felt something behind him – Arturo was already there.

'Who is it?' Walli whispered.

'That British girl,' Arturo squeaked.

'I know you are in there!' Dandelion screamed. 'Come out before I kick down the door and use it to batter your brains all the way to Pictland!'

'Can she do that?' Walli whined.

'I think so,' Arturo nodded glumly.

'Wait a moment,' Walli called out. His hands were shaking so much he had trouble pulling the wooden bolt across. The door swung open and Dandelion barged in, her face sunrise red with fury.

'Where's our cow?' she demanded.

'Your cow?' Walli asked.

'Are you deaf or daft?' the girl snapped. 'Cow. Big animal, horns on head, grass in one end, cowpats out the other end and milk in the middle. Brown in colour. Cow.'

'Yes, I know what a cow is, little girl…'

Dandelion went still as a statue. She reached across to Walli's belt and slid out the short sword. She raised the point until it was under the soldier's nose.

'No, lit … er … Miss Dandelion.'

'Princess Dandelion.'

'What?'

'My Ma is Queen Virago so that makes me a princess, doesn't it?' she asked sweetly and pushed the sword tip just a little way up Walli's nose.

'Yes lit … Your Majesty!' Walli said.

'Now,' Dandelion said, still in that voice – quiet as an adder in the moors but twice as deadly. 'Last night we had a cow tied to a stake in the field near our village. This morning I went to get some milk for my porridge and the cow was gone.'

'Escaped?' Arturo said.

'Stolen,' Dandelion said.

Arturo nodded hard. 'Yes, Captain Obnoctius warned us the Brits were a band of thieves! Hah! Don't trust them a Roman perch, he said.'

Perch is a Roman measure – so don't trust the Brits out of your sight. A perch is also the thing a parrot sits on in a cage. Don't get them mixed up. When Arturo said, 'Don't trust them a perch,' he didn't mean, 'Don't lend them your parrot or they'll eat it.' Though he might have done. Best not to risk your lovely parrot.

Dandelion removed the sword tip from Walli's nostril and placed it gently on the top of Arturo's nose. 'The British are the truest and most honest people you Romans would ever wish to meet…'

'We're Gaul,' Arturo reminded her and the sword point vanished half a perch up his nose. 'Sorry, Your Majesty!' he squawked.

Dandelion went on, 'The Picts must have stolen it,' she said calmly. 'There is a pigging great wall between us and them. So they must have come in during the night through a gate. Where is the nearest gate?'

'Here, Your Majesty.'

'And who was supposed to be guarding it?'

'Walli,' Arturo said. 'It was his turn, Princess, honest. He probably fell asleep on duty – he's always doing that. Captain Obnoctius said he'd have him stoned to death if it ever happened again. And he will when I tell him.'

'Thank you,' Walli muttered bitterly.

Dandelion suddenly gave a great grin! 'Wonderful! That will save my Ma the trouble of roasting you slowly over our hearth fire. We can tell the Captain his men are to blame, get a new cow from the Roman Army ... and we can all come to watch the stoning. In fact we may even join in. I've heard small stones are best because death is slower. Your skin is slowly ripped from your body ... unless you get a pebble in the eye and...'

'Stop!' Walli wailed. 'Stop! Please don't tell Obnoctius. I'm sorry, really sorry!'

Dandelion shrugged and handed him back his sword.

'Sorry doesn't get me milk for my porridge. Sorry doesn't get our cow back!'

'We'll get your cow back,' Walli promised. 'We'll wait till dark and raid the Pictish camp. There are just women and children there.'

'What do you mean just women?' Dandelion asked softly.

'I mean ... not trained warriors...' Walli laughed shakily.

'What do you mean just children?' the girl asked.

'I ... I ... I mean ... just Pict children – not brave Amazons like a British princess,' he said with a trembly smile.

'What's an Amazon?' dandelion asked.

'A Roman legend says there were a tribe of warrior women – the Amazons. The Roman Army fought them. The Roman men wanted to capture them as wives,' Arturo explained.

Dandelion prodded him in the breastplate with a firm finger. It hurt, even through the armour. 'Remember what Boudica did to the Romans? That's what my Ma is like and I am just the same. So get our cow back or die with your Roman friend here,' she said.

'Can't do that,' Arturo said with a big sigh. 'It's my turn to stay on guard. If I desert the Milecastle and get caught I'll be executed. I could be thrown into a bed of nettles and left to be stung to death.

Yes this was another really rotless Roman punishment. Would you like to be thrown into a nettle bed? It's not like a petal bed. You couldn't settle, lettle lone be in fine fettle ... unless you were wearing a suit of metal.

'Tell you what though,' Arturo continued, grinning his handsome Gaullish grin. 'Walli is free tonight – and it's his fault because he fell asleep – Walli will go and get your cow back!'

'Will he?'

'No ... Walli.'

Walli looked worried. 'Alone?'

The girl scowled. 'No. You are too stupid. You need a warrior princess alongside you. I'll go with you. I'll be back at sunset and we will raid the Picts and rescue Music.'

'What?'

'The cow – we call her Music because she's a moo and when she eats rotten corn she is sick. Moo-sick, geddit?'

The Gauls laughed feebly.

'Till sunset,' Dandelion said and swept out of the guard room as grandly as her spindly short legs would allow.

She went back to porridge made with water. She was not a happy child ... sorry, I meant to say she was not a happy princess.

***

Walli wore two pairs of trousers to keep out the cold. Dandelion went bare-legged as she always did.

They stepped out of the milecastle gate into the marshy wastes of Pictland. There were too many clouds to see the moon and stars but the sky behind the Pictish hill glowed red and golden sparks rose into the night sky.

Roman wall-guards could see the glow from twenty miles away. It could have been a raid, burning down a village. 'Good!' they sniggered nastily. 'A roasted Pict is a good Pict! Hah! We're not going over to find out ... not in the dark, anyway.'

Dandelion turned her head sharply at every sound in the reedy grass, afraid the Pict guards would see her and Walli. But there didn't seem to be anyone on guard tonight. The bright firelight would have shown up anyone standing on top of the hill. Nothing. No one.

'We'll look over the top of the hill and see what's going on,' Dandelion told the soldier. 'But as soon as we look over our faces will be lit by the fire. Take your helmet off or the light will shine on it.'

'Me head'll get cold!' Walli gasped.

'Not as cold as it'll be when it's been lopped off and is lying in the grass,' the girl reminded him. 'Now get on your hands and knees,' she ordered.

'I'll dirty my knees! These are my best trousers.'

Dandelion didn't bother to answer. She just fixed her fierce eyes on him. Even on the dark side of the hill he felt the stare. He dropped to his hands and knees.

As they came close to the top of the hill they could hear shouting and singing. The Pict women and children must have been making ale and become drunk, Dandelion decided. The song drifted over through the smoky air...

'We are the Scots and we are the Picts,
We steal the British cattle and we never get nicked.
We are the army in the woollen kilts,
We stick our swords in Britons right up to the hilt.'

41

There was a massive cheer … but there was something odd about the sound. Walli wasn't sure what it was. But Dandelion knew at once.

'Men!' she whispered. 'The McKilt tribe have men.'

'So?'

'So … so the Romans arrested them all and sent them off to fight somewhere in the Empire. Maggie McKilt has brought more in … maybe hired warriors from another tribe. The Attacotti, probably.'

'Attacotti? They eat people, don't they?' Walli panted.

'Oh, it's all right, they don't eat people with dirty knees,' she told him.

'Oh, good,' he said, relieved.

The girl shook her head. 'How did you Romans ever beat us Britons?' she asked.

'I'm a Gaul,' he said.

She ignored his answer. 'If they are bringing in soldiers they must be planning an attack. They probably want to kidnap the women the way the Romans did with those Hammy-zons. So my Ma will have to bring in some Brigante soldiers to help us. It'll mean war!'

Walli raised a finger in the air. 'Excuse me, Princess, but you are forgetting the Roman Army is standing between you. We won't let you fight a war. In fact Captain Obnoctius said we'd keep the peace or die trying.'

'Then you'll die,' Dandelion said. 'The Picts will climb the Wall and cut your throats while you sleep on guard duty. Then they'll open the gates and rush through to kidnap us.'

Walli kneeled proud and tall. 'We'll stop them!' he promised.

'The way you stopped them stealing our cow last night?'

'Yes,' he said. Then, 'Oh.'

Dandelion shuffled on. 'We need to get Music back,' she said. 'If they are drinking ale they'll fall fast asleep before long. When the fire dies down we'll find the cow and take her home.'

'We will,' Walli agreed.

Dandelion peered over the hill. 'We won't,' she groaned.

'We won't?'

'That isn't a campfire. It's a cooking fire. Look,' she said.

Walli stretched his neck to look over the brow of the hill. A fire was crackling and sparking in a fire pit. The sweet smell of fresh roasting flesh drifted on the northerly wind and made him hungry. Over the pit there was a wooden frame. Hanging on the frame was the body of a large animal. As the flesh roasted, the Pict men and women were carving slices of meat off it, stuffing it in their mouths and washing it down with cups of ale.

'Our poor old Music,' Dandelion wailed. 'First we'll starve half to death without Music's milk and then they'll attack. We'll be too weak to fight back. Stealing the cow was all part of their plan ... and it's all your fault,' she told Walli.

'Sorry,' he muttered miserably.

'Not as sorry as you'll be when we use the last of our strength to stone you to death,' she promised.

Now Dandelion was a clever girl. She was right that the Picts had caught and roasted Music the cow to feast on. But she was wrong about the Pictish plot to murder their way across the Wall.

And even clever Dandelion couldn't see into the future. She couldn't see what would happen next morning to change the tale of terror.

No one could see it coming...

The Romans had soothsayers who said they could see into the future. They were frauds and fakes. Then there were the priests who fed holy chickens – they said they could see if the Romans will be lucky or not from the way the chickens peck at their corn. Lucky? Hah! More like clucky.

KICKS, COALS
AND COWS

Don McKilt was bored. There was no one to play with. The rest of the McKilt tribe and the warriors were snoring loud enough to shake the turf roofs on the huts. After all they'd eaten and drunk last night they would sleep till noon.

And Don wanted to play because Don had his new toy.

When he brought home the stolen cow he was a hero in the Pict village. With the help of the McGargle brothers he'd simply cut the cow's rope and led it back through the milecastle gate. Don had closed the doors and barred them again once the cow was through. Then he'd climbed back over to the Pict side. Of course, when he told the tale, he made it sound much more dangerous.

'The McGargles helped, though,' their granny Jinny argued.

Don sniffed. 'They kept watch, I suppose,' he sighed and the wee warriors nodded quietly. Don had done the dangerous part. He was promised the best bit of the dead animal.

'Do you want a steak?' the warriors' cook had asked.

'No, I don't want a steak,' Don said.

'Do you want a piece of juicy liver?'

'No, I don't want liver.'

'Do you want its eyes?'

'No, I don't want its eyes.'

'What do you want?'

'I want its belly,' Don said.

The cook nodded wisely. 'When I was your age I'd have said just the same. I'll bring it to you when I've gutted the animal and washed it out,' he promised.

It was growing dark when the cook presented Don with the belly of the cow. It was trimmed neatly and one end tied up. Don grinned happily. He blew into the open tube at the other end. When it was fat and firm he tied the end and held it in his hands.

Don stepped into the patch of grass between the huts, dropped the blown-up belly and kicked it. The belly bounced in a wobbly sort of way and came back off the wall of a hut. He kicked it over and over again – when it came back high he hit it with his head.

At last the woman who lived in the hut came out with her dagger and screamed at him, 'If you don't stop kicking that ball against my wall I will cut it into strips of tripe. You're giving me a right headache.'

'Aw go soak your head in the sea, Jinny McGargle,' Don shouted back … but he knew she meant it. The ball was put away safely while he went to share in the feast that night.

In the morning he'd have a game of ball-foot with the warriors and it would be the best time he'd had since his Pa was taken away by the Romans. Pa had taught Don to make a ball and play. He missed him.

But when morning came the warriors were snoring and Don's ball was crying out to be kicked. He couldn't kick it against the huts any more, so he wandered to the top of the hill and looked over the swampy ground. Then he saw it. The answer to a young boy's dream.

The Wall! The Wall of the rotten Romans. An ugly great slab that made Pictland a prison. But perfect for a game of kickies!

He splashed through the marshy grass till he reached the Wall. The idiot guards weren't in sight. He started kicking the ball against the Wall. The rough stones sent it spinning in odd ways and it was much more fun than playing against a hut wall.

He stopped for a moment, panting, then picked up a piece of black stone – the sort that burned well on a fire. What did his Ma, Maggie McKilt, call these stones? Coal, that was it. He walked over to the wall and scratched black, coaly lines on the light stone wall. It was a rough square just a little higher than a man. A target to hit … or miss.

He placed the ball on the same spot and aimed for the target to see how many he could score out of ten. He managed five the first time.

'Five points to me ... five to the Romans,' he laughed.
'No. "Points" is a daft British word. I'll have a new name ...
I'll name it after the black stone! Yes, it's five coals to me!'

And as years passed football scores were known as 'coals' ... but
half-deaf people call them 'goals'. I hope you believe me. It took
me a long time to think of that story.

He placed the ball on its spot again and kicked it hard
against the Wall. This time it caught a join between the
stones and bounced upwards. Don ran forward and
decided to try a new trick – he'd hit the ball with his head
and score a coal with a header.

He ran forward, looking up at the ball swirling in the
Pictish wind. That's why he didn't see the rock on the
ground. He tripped at the last moment and the ball hit the
top of his head and soared upwards. The wind caught it
and carried it to the top of the Wall. It bounced and
vanished over to the British side.

If Don hadn't been a young warrior he'd have burst
into tears. Instead he wiped his nose on the back of his
hand and sniffed ... without quite crying.

'I've got to get it back,' he said fiercely.

Don ran back to the Pict village and into his hut.

Maggie McKilt was snoring under her bearskin rug.
He pulled out the rope with a hook and sped back to the
Wall. Walli was wandering miserably around the milecastle
tower so Don had to trot along to where the Wall dipped

and curved out of his sight.

The hook caught in the top of the Wall and he began to pull himself up. He peered over the top. The British villagers were gathering in the village on the far side of the road that ran on their side of the Wall. There was a lot of angry shouting. He couldn't hear what they were saying but guessed they were upset by the loss of their cow. And his guess was right.

Don walked along the Wall towards the tower and the spot where he thought the ball might be.

Then things started to happen quickly.

He saw the ball and realized he'd left his rope dangling on the Pict side. He couldn't jump down without breaking a few bones. He'd have to go closer to the milecastle and use the stairs.

He heard an angry cry and noticed that the British tribe were marching towards the Wall. At first he thought they were going to attack the shivering Gaul guards at the top of one of the towers. Then he saw Queen Virago at the head of the group was pointing upwards ... and she was pointing straight at him. 'That's one of the Pict brats. They roasted Music – we'll roast him!'

The women and children ran to the stairway by the milecastle. Walli stood firm at the top and barred their way. But when Queen Virago was just two steps from the top he lost his nerve, turned and ran inside the tower.

Little Don also turned and ran but he ran back towards where his rope hung over the Wall. He saw a strange figure walking towards him from the Roman fort. A very small man with a very large crest on his helmet marching towards him and blowing into an invisible trumpet,

'Par-parp-a-parp-parp! Par-parp-a-parp-parp!'

When the little Roman officer saw Don he stopped and drew his sword. He had stopped just beside the Pict boy's rope and had cut off his escape.

'Aha! A raider. Know what we do with raiders? We crucify them alive along the road into Rome ... or in your case the road into Wallsend.'

To step forward was certain death ... to run back was to run into the horde of British women ... and almost certain death.

GET HIM!

GRAB HIM!

GUT HIM!

Don ran towards the women. They snatched at him with hard, clawing hands and bound him with their belts.

'Bring that boy back here!' Obnoctius cried.

The British women bundled Don down the stairs, over the road, across the mound and into their village. Virago took long slow steps towards the Roman Captain. She smiled a gap-toothed grin that she thought made her look gorgeous. 'But big, brave, strong and handsome Captain,' she said in a voice like silk ... rough silk ... 'it was just one of our children trying to play on your love-erly, wuvverly wall. We'll take him back to the villy-willage and punish him. After all, we are Rome's bestest friendy-wendies. We can't have you upsetty-wetty, can we?'

'He was wearing a kilt ... he's a Pict!' Obnoctius squeaked.

'He was playing at Picts and Brits – it was his turn to be the baddie,' Virago explained.

She raised a hand and scratched Obnoctius gently under the chin. 'Urk!' he squawked.

'And since you've sent our dear husbands to fight overseas we are so lonely, you know. We are always pleased to see handsome young men like you in our village!' She gave a very fat wink that made Obnoctius blink. 'Know what I mean?'

Well, you'd blink if you were blasted with Virago's stinking breath. Toothpaste hadn't been invented by the Britons. It is said the Romans made tooth-cleaner from powdered mouse brains. That's a fact. So I will not make some feeble joke about their teeth being squeaky clean.

He managed to nod. She waved her fingers under his nose. 'Bye-ee!'

Obnoctius watched her stride back down the stairway by the tower and cross to the village. Then he turned and walked back towards the fort. After a dozen paces he stopped. 'I forgot why I was coming to the milecastle!' he muttered. 'But while I'm here I'll give those two idle guards a good beating. Letting a little British boy on to the Wall. Where were they? Why didn't they stop him?'

And a minute later he was asking the same thing to the worried faces of Walli and Arturo. 'Sorry, Captain,' Walli whined.

'What if the boy had fallen off the Wall? Eh?' the Captain demanded.

'Is that a trick question?' Walli wondered.

'Well? What if he'd fallen off?'

'He'd have hurt himself?' the guard asked.

'He'd have killed himself, you clown – but the point is, the point I am making, the point you should be thinking is this … the British would be angry. They would want revenge for a careless couple of guards. They would probably want to kill you. I would have to march out with a troop from the fort and save your lives.'

'Thank you, sir.'

'Then I would have to take you back to the fort and have you stoned to death.'

'Thank you, sir.'

'Now go through the fields and bring back as many large stones as you can find. I want them piled up beside the catapult so it is ready to beat off a Pict attack. Last

53

night there were fires burning in the village over the hill. Those Pict women are up to something. Planning a revolt probably!'

'No, just roasting a cow,' Walli said.

Arturo gave him a sharp kick on the leg to silence him.

'We never left our guard posts last night,' he hissed.

'Ah.' Walli nodded. 'Sorry, sir. Maybe they are preparing a feast for Adrian's visit the same as Queen Virago is on the British side.'

'Hadrian's visit?' Obnoctius cried. 'Hadrian is coming here? Our noble emperor has heard about my wonderful work in stopping the war and he is coming to present me with a golden laurel crown himself! Oh, joy!' the Captain sighed and turned to run back to the fort.

'But, sir, I'm not sure they'd be preparing a feast for Emperor Hadrian, would they? I mean…'

But Obnoctius had rushed out of the tower and vanished on the road back to the fort. 'Par-parp-a-parp-parp! Par-parp-a-parp-parp!'

Yes, dear reader, the Emperor Hadrian had been dead for over 50 years. But, when you get as excited as Obnoctius was, you forget little things like that. You'd be just the same, believe me.

***

In a small hut in the British village Virago and Dandelion looked at the bound and gagged boy.

'Can I kill him, Ma?' Dandelion asked softly.

54

'Oh, no, Princess,' her mother said. 'This young hostage is Maggie McKilt's own dear son. He is worth much, much more alive.'

'Aw … can't I kill him even a little bit?' the girl groaned.

'It'll cost the powerless Picts at least ten cows to get him back.'

'I could give him a good kicking,' Dandelion offered.

'When we get our cows, Dandelion. When we get our cows.'

The boy's eyes glared at her. Dandelion smiled an evil smile. 'Oh, good,' she said. 'Oh, good.'

ROCKS, REVENGE AND ROMANS

Walli worked hard all morning carrying stones from the fields and piling them up beside the mighty catapult.

'Aren't you going to carry any?' he asked Arturo.

'No,' the blond Gaul told his little partner. 'This is a team effort. I find them, you carry them.'

'So can we swap? I find them and you carry them?' Walli asked.

'No. My hands are too soft for that sort of work. They would be torn and bleeding in no time at all ... I wouldn't be fit to throw a spear or fight with a sword. That would make Obnoctius angry. And we don't want that, Walli, do we?'

Walli plodded on till the pile of stones was as high as he was. They stopped to eat some dried fish and bread at noon.

> Dried fish is not the tastiest dish you'd wish for. But they were a long way from the sea. YOU'D be dry by the time you got from the sea to Milecastle 13. So if the fish was dry you can't blame it. So stop at once. The fish was innocent.

The Wall sheltered them from the cruel Pictish wind and the spring sunshine was almost warm as they sat with their backs to the catapult to eat.

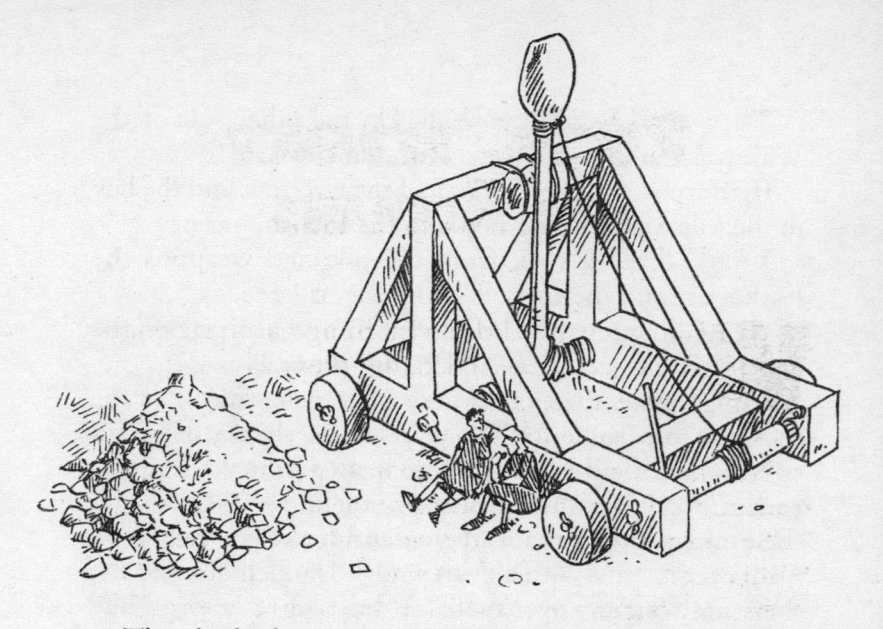

They looked up to see Queen Virago and her daughter Dandelion striding towards them. 'Hello, Princess,' Walli said wearily. 'More trouble?'

Dandelion gave an evil grin. 'I see the stones are all piled up, ready to stone you to death?'

'No, they are for firing into the Pict village if they try to make trouble,' Arturo said.

Virago nodded. 'So they can also be used to fire a message into the village,' she said.

'I suppose so. But what's the use of that? I don't think the Picts can read,' Arturo argued.

'That's why we are sending them a picture instead of a written message.' The British Queen unrolled a patch of leather. She had used a burnt stick to draw a boy in a kilt with a British queen holding a knife to his throat.

They stood beside the Wall. On the other side of the Wall was the Pictish Queen with ten cows.

In the next picture Virago had the ten cows and the boy in the kilt was running home to the Pictish queen.

Virago lifted a rock from the pile and wrapped the leather around the rock. 'Fire it,' she ordered.

'The Captain would be upset if he saw us firing on the Picts without his orders,' Walli said miserably.

Virago gave a shrug. 'So open the gates and take the message to Maggie McKilt yourself ... she's a witch, of course, and she'll either spill your guts to make a magic spell ... that's what the druids do, you know? Or she'll get the Pict warriors to capture you and make you her slave. Oh, yes,' she said with a grim smile. 'Dandelion's told me there are warriors over there. At least ten ... a weed like you couldn't fight them.'

Walli sighed. 'We'll send the message in the catapult.' His arms were tired from carrying heavy stones all morning but with Virago's powerful hands to help, he wound back the arm of the machine. The Queen lifted the message on the stone into the bowl at the end of the catapult's throwing arm.

Arturo pulled the pin that held the arm and it flew upwards with a clatter. They stood and watched as the stone soared into the noonday sun.

***

Maggie McKilt had a sore head and a mouth that tasted like she'd chewed a cowpat.

Not that she made a habit of chewing cowpats, you understand. But from time to time she would gather dried cow droppings to burn on the fires in her hut. She would then pick up a lump of bread and stuff it into her mouth without washing her hands ... well, you don't need me to go on, do you?

She rolled off her pile of sheep fleeces and put on her warmest woollen dress and cloak. She blinked out into the sunlight. 'Water!' she croaked. There was no one to answer her order. The warriors were still snoring in their hut. 'Where's my Don?' she grumbled as she made her way to a stream that ran at the back of the village.

The villagers used it as a toilet so she chose a spot upstream to dip a leather bucket in and draw out some icy water. She splashed the water on her face and shuddered before carrying the bucket back to her house.

'I'll teach the idle little toad,' she said as she stumbled through the door into the dark room. 'Are you getting out of bed, you little slug?' she cried. When there was no reply she tipped the freezing water on to Don's bed and waited for his squawks of shock.

Nothing. Maggie dropped the bucket and felt the bed. It was empty – very damp, but empty. 'Where's the little whelp gone?' she muttered.

She went back to the doorway and screamed, 'Don! Get yourself here at once!' The turf roofs trembled at her voice and sleepers stirred and began to rise. Bleary-eyed faces appeared at doorways. 'Have you seen my son?'

their Queen demanded.

One woman groaned, 'He's probably away with that blasted football – I told him not to kick it against my cottage. He'll be on the moors.'

Maggie McKilt snorted, 'You're a sour-faced hen, Jinny McGargle. Sending my poor little boy away from the safety of the village.'

A small boy stuck his head out under Jinny's arm. 'I think Don might have gone to the Wall, Queen Maggie,' he said. 'He likes to play ball-foot when he gets the chance and the Wall would be a great place for a kick-about.'

Maggie scowled and turned towards the Wall.

It's just as well she did. Because at that moment she saw something spinning through the air towards her. Her mouth fell open in wonder and terror. At the last moment she ducked and the stone crashed into the ground, went through the curtain at the doorway to her hut and hurtled inside. It bounced once and smashed its way through the far wall before rolling to a stop by the warriors' hut.

The Queen hated her tribe to see her afraid. She tugged fiercely at her cloak and raised her fists. 'War!' she raged. 'This means war. They are using their Roman friends and their machines to attack us. War!'

By now the villagers were staggering out of their huts and the warriors too. They gathered around their raging Queen. 'They are too afraid to fight us face to face. They try sneaky tricks like firing rocks…'

'It was a bit sneaky stealing their cow,' Jinny McGargle told her. 'This will be a revenge attack. I said it was a nasty trick to play.'

'We were hungry – I was feeding you, you wretch!' Queen Maggie ranted. 'Don't be grateful to me or my brave son Don ... oh, don't be grateful, you two-eyed hag!'

'What's wrong with having two eyes?' Jinny asked.

'What's wrong with it? Don't ask stupid questions. Now get your weapons and climbing ropes. We attack at dawn!'

'It's noon already,' Jinny told her. 'You're a bit late. Anyway, they'll be ready for us. They'll chop us down as soon as we try to climb the Wall.'

'I know that! I know that! I know that!' Maggie screamed. 'We'll wait till dark and attack tomorrow at dawn ... get your weapons sharp and ready. Say your prayers and burn some of that cow to our gods. We go to death or glory!'

'Excuse me, Queen Maggie,' one of the warriors said quietly. He was tall and thin and dark-skinned. He had a handsome face. What was odd, for a Pict, was that it was a very clean face. Almost as if he had washed it. Most odd.

'What?' Maggie snarled.

'That stone seems to have a message wrapped around it. Maybe the British weren't attacking,' the warrior said. Maggie McKilt sighed. 'Don't be stupid, Marco. They would not send a message when they know I can't read.'

'Maybe they know we can read,' he said pointing at his men. 'Maybe they know who we are.'

'Well don't stand there catching butterflies with your open mouth, man. Let's see what they have to say.'

Marco unwrapped the leather and held the message against the wall so the village could see it. Maggie began to read the pictures. 'Boy with knife to throat ... that looks like Virago with a knife to my Don's throat. My boy! They've captured my son. That's why he's disappeared.' She moaned. 'So? What do the ten cows mean?'

Marco peered at it. 'Ten cows in exchange for the boy,' Marco said.

'That's madness,' Maggie spat. 'Where would I get ten cows?'

'Steal them ... the way your husband used to before the Romans took him,' Jinny McGargle said.

Maggie sucked some strands of last night's cow meat through her crooked teeth. 'Either that or rescue Don.'

'We'd need to get over the Wall and back again ... fight the Romans and the British,' Marco said. 'If we got it wrong they'd cut Don's throat before we could save him. And we could all end up on the wrong side of the Wall.'

'That's right,' one of the warriors said. 'It could all be a trap just to get us on the British side.'

The men muttered and agreed.

'So,' Maggie said fiercely, 'Are you refusing to help me when I need it? After I helped you?'

The warriors shuffled their feet and looked miserable. Marco said, 'Not refusing, exactly ... I just think we need to be careful. See if there's any way round this.'

'Round this?'

'Anything else they'll do to set Don free. The last thing we want to do is get into a fight with the Roman Army. We said we'd help you raid the Britons and even fight them ... but you know why we don't want to fight the Romans...'

'Because you are cowards,' Maggie sneered. 'Because you have all the heart of that chicken over there. Because you are not real warriors, you are just squirming little polecats with swords.'

The Queen turned to her tribe. 'Our brave warriors here don't want to fight. But my women will go into battle for me, won't they?' she cried.

The women looked at one another. 'No, Maggie, we won't,' Jinny said quietly. 'Don got himself into trouble. We have our own children to worry about – we can't all risk our lives for one boy.' The other women nodded. 'Our children come first. We know the men can't fight the Romans and we know why. It's down to you to do something about Don if you want to save his skin.'

The warriors and the tribe turned back to their huts to get ready for a day's work in the fields or seeing to their sheep or hunting for supper.

Maggie McKilt had never felt so lonely in her life.

'I don't need you ... you ... you traitors. McKilts forever!' she cried. But the tribe had closed their ears.

Maggie may have felt a bit better if she could only have seen what was happening on the other side of the Wall at that very moment...

***

Virago stood on the mound of the vallum. 'Tomorrow night we will feast on tender Pictish cow and drink sweet Pictish cow milk,' she promised her people.

'But what will you do with the boy?' a woman asked.

'Send him back ... fire him in the catapult!' Virago laughed.

'After I've given him a kicking,' Dandelion added.

The women of the village shook their heads. 'I know the Picts took our Music and ate her – but a cow's just a cow. You can't go kidnapping kids in revenge,' a grey-haired, older woman said quietly. 'It's not right.'

Virago's eyes burned angrily. 'Those who are not with me are against me!' she cried and waved her short, Roman sword.

The villagers nodded. 'Then we're against you, Virago,' they said and walked away.

'Traitors!' Virago screamed.

It sounded like an echo from the other side of the Wall.

The Queens were two stubborn women. Neither would give way even half a perch. They were on the road to war between the two tribes … again.

But they were forgetting about the Romans standing between them…

HIPPOS, HOPPOS AND HELEFLUMPS

'Par-parp-a-parp-parp! Par-parp-a-parp-parp!'
Obnoctius marched along the Wall.

This time the troop's trumpeter marched in front of him and it was a real trumpet blast that made Walli and Arturo race back to their post at the Milecastle.

The trumpeter wheezed and puffed and stumbled to the tower door. It isn't easy marching along the cobbled path at the top of the Wall and playing the trumpet at the same time.

Obnoctius stood at the top of the steps that led down from the tower. He ordered Arturo and Walli to stand in front of him on the stairs, two steps down so he had a guard of honour – but not a guard that made him look small.

The British women and children stopped at the mound and wandered back to the Wall to see what was going on. 'People of Britain!' Obnoctius cried. 'Greetings from the mighty Roman Army.'

No one greeted him back. The women just stared and the smallest children hid behind their skirts.

'I bring great news,' Obnoctius went on. 'As you know the Emperor Hadrian is making a visit to the Wall.'

'Hadrian's dead!' Virago called back.

Obnoctius turned red and bellowed even louder. 'Dead! Dead? How could a dead man build a wall, you quaint Queen?'

'He didn't build the Wall. He just ordered the army to build it with the help of the British. He never even visited it!'

'Ah ... yes ... well ... he's going to visit it now!' Obnoctius told her.

School pupils used to trick their teacher with this quick question. 'Where is Hadrian's Wall?' Answer: 'At the bottom of Hadrian's garden.' Of course you would never read such a dreadful joke in a Horrible Histories book.

'He's dead!' the British women shouted back with one voice.

'We'll see about that!' Obnoctius said. 'And when he arrives I want to show him how well his brilliant Wall works. How it keeps out the barbarians and shelters you from them...'

'It didn't save our cow,' Virago laughed bitterly.

Obnoctius wasn't listening. ' ...and how much you Britons love the Romans being here.' Obnoctius drew his sword and slapped the trumpeter who was leaning, exhausted, against the tower door. 'Give me a fanfare!'

'Par-parp-a-parp-parp! Par-parp-a-phuttttt!' was the best the poor man could manage.

'So, dear Britons, here is my great plan ... we will entertain the Emperor the way he would be entertained in Rome ... with games, gladiators and a feast!'

The women shrugged and one cried, 'We've never seen Roman games.'

'And we haven't a clue what Romans like to eat ... even if we had any spare food.'

'Fear not!' Obnoctius cried and he felt his throat going a little sore from all the shouting. He walked down the steps and pushed Walli and Arturo into leading him across to the catapult. He stood on the frame and the women and children gathered round. 'As I was saying,' he said in a softer voice. 'Fear not ... my troops will help you and my fort will help with the food. First the games...'

'Sounds fun,' Dandelion nodded.

Obnoctius almost fell off the catapult. 'Fun?' he gasped. 'Fun? There is nothing fun about Roman games, young lady. They are the most serious events there are ... more serious than war. There is nothing fun about gladiators fighting to the death, criminals being executed slowly and cruelly or animals being butchered for sport. The games are serious ... deadly serious.'

Virago sat on the ground and the other women and

children joined her. 'Fighting to the death sounds fun to me. So tell us some more, Captain.'

Obnoctius puffed out his chest as far as his breastplate would let him and stared south into the sun as if he could see Rome from where he stood.

In a way he could see Rome. He could see it in his head. This is because Obnoctius was a little potty. No. I am lying. Obnoctius was totally potty.

'The games in Rome take place in a wonderful building called the Colosseum. Fifty thousand people gather in the morning to watch...'

'We haven't got fifty thousand in the whole of North Britain ... and we haven't time to build a Colosseum, Captain,' a woman reminded the Roman.

'We can hold the games here ... with the Wall on the north and the mound to the south. In fact you can sit on the mound and ... yes, I have a wonderful idea ... we can invite the Picts to sit on the Wall. It'll make a bigger crowd.'

The women looked worried at the thought. 'You'll bring more troops to keep an eye on them ... stop them bringing weapons or attacking us, won't you?' Virago asked.

'I will,' Obnoctius said. His gaze drifted south again. 'In the morning we have the venatores, the animal hunts. In Carthage they say a man fought to the death against an elephant. I've seen packs of dogs hunt rhinos and men armed with clubs face raging bears. Sometimes we get animals to fight each other – wild boars against bears, lions against crocodiles.'

'There aren't a lot of crocodiles in…' Virago began to object but Obnoctius wasn't listening.

'Then, at noon, we have dinner while criminals are being executed. Sometimes we throw a Christian to a leopard. Or we tie a thief to the belly of a boar and let it rip at him with its sharp tusks. Sometimes we kill them in a new and interesting way … I've seen a man tied to a post. His mouth was forced open and boiling lead poured down his throat. Some are thrown off a high cliff,' he went on.

'We could throw someone off the Wall,' Dandelion suggested.

'Maybe we can think of a new way to kill someone to make Hadrian happy?' Obnoctius muttered.

'Put them in the catapult and fire them at the Wall!' Dandelion cried. 'I know just the boy I'd like to do that to,' she giggled.

'Hush,' her mother warned her. 'The officer doesn't know we've kidnapped a Pict.'

Dandelion sighed.

'I like that idea,' Obnoctius smiled. 'You can arrange it. Now, as I was saying, that's how they pass their lunch break in Rome. And, in the afternoon, we have the fights between the gladiators. Sword fights between Dimacheri – as we call them … or men with forks and nets – what we call Retiarii. And sometimes we have comical fights where both gladiators are blindfolded … Andabatae. We can have them all!'

'Excuse me, Captain,' Virago interrupted. 'But where

do we find the gladiators?'

'What?'

'We are thousands of miles from Rome. Where will we get gladiators?'

Before Obnoctius could answer another woman asked, 'Not to mention hoppos!'

'Hippos,' the Roman said.

'Hippos, then ... and heleflumps ...'

'Elephants.'

'All right ... hippos and elephants and panters.'

'Panthers.'

'In fact where do we get the criminals to execute?' Virago asked.

The other women joined in with a flood of questions and Obnoctius had to wave to the trumpeter for a blast to silence them. 'Par-parp-a-parp-parp! Par-parp-a-phuttttt!'

At last it was quiet. Obnoctius said, 'We will make do with what we have. Let's start with the animal hunts. You have wolves in this country, don't you?'

'Yes, but you won't find anyone who'll go out and try to catch one alive,' Dandelion said. 'We kill them when they attack our sheep and goats.'

'Aha!' the captain cried. 'Sheep and goats! We can have a sheep hunt.'

Walli and Arturo looked at one another. 'Captain, sir,' Walli said, 'it's not quite the same as a crocodile hunt, is it?' 'It's a start,' Obnoctius said. 'And the sheep around here have very nasty horns.'

This is still true. Sheep at the Wall are still vicious things. Never get into a fight with one – ewe can't bleat them.

'But who can we execute at noon?' a woman asked.

'Leave that to us,' Virago said and winked at her daughter.

'Yes,' Dandelion nodded. 'It will be a pleasure to put him on the catapult and fire him at the Wall ... the very Wall his Ma will be sitting on, watching!' She giggled till it hurt and she rolled on the soft grass clutching her sides.

'We still don't have any gladiators!' the woman moaned again.

'Well, Queen Virago here is a warrior queen,' Obnoctius smiled. 'The Colosseum does have women gladiators from time to time. If one of you other women would care to fight her we have a contest worthy of Rome!'

The women gave a gasp. 'Fight Virago!' one hissed.

'Are you mad? She doesn't fight fair.'

'I fight fairly fair,' Virago grumbled.

The woman stood up and jabbed a finger in the Queen's direction. 'You kick, you scratch, you bite and you spit!'

'Only when I'm losing,' Virago argued.

'You punch people in the mouth, you bend their fingers back and you chew at their ears.'

'Only if I get upset and lose my temper,' the Queen snapped.

'You jump up and down on heads and you gouge eyes with your thumbs and you...'

'All right! All right, Bella, you have made your point. The problem is who can we find to fight me?' she asked.

72

'Anyone want to give it a try?'

The women shuffled away in case Virago picked one.

'I'll take it easy,' she promised. 'No biting?'

No reply.

'I'll fight with one hand tied behind by back!'

Bella looked down at the grass and murmured, 'You'd be better off picking on a Pict.'

Virago's face split in a broken-toothed grin. 'Perfect, Bella, perfect! Why didn't I think of that? I'll fight the evil Maggie McKilt.'

Dandelion jumped to her feet. 'And Don McKilt will be the prize. He'll be loaded into the catapult to watch the fight. If his Ma wins he goes free ... if we win we fire the catapult and splatter him against the Wall. That's better than any boring old gladiator fight!'

Obnoctius nodded. 'The Emperor would like that. Will Queen Maggie accept the challenge?'

'Oh, yes.' Virago nodded. Out of the side of her mouth she muttered to Dandelion, 'She has no choice – it's her only chance to save her son.'

The Roman turned to Walli. 'You can carry the challenge across to the Queen of the Picts.'

'Me!' Walli squeaked. 'Why me?'

'Because it is against the law for a Briton to pass through the Wall. The penalty is to be torn apart by dogs. No, the Picts will not harm a messenger from Rome – they wouldn't dare.' Obnoctius jumped down from the catapult and began to walk quickly back and forth. 'Tell them the games start an hour before noon. The gates will open and we will allow their tribe to sit on the Wall and watch. At

73

noon we put this boy prisoner ... what's his name?'

'Don,' Dandelion said.

'Is that the boy in the skirt I caught this morning?' he asked.

'That's the one,' Virago agreed.

'He deserves to die. We put him in the catapult and then have the contest between the queens ... the winner gets to pull the pin and fire the boy from the catapult. If Queen Maggie wins, she'll enjoy that.'

'No she won't,' Dandelion sniggered softly.

'Off you go, trooper Walachia,' the captain ordered. 'I will start teaching these British women how to prepare a Roman feast.'

Old Bella shook her head. 'Two feasts,' she muttered.

'One for our Adrian and one for the Roman Emperor. Wassisname?'

'Hadrian,' her friend told her.

'No, that's our visitor, Adrian.'

'He's called Hadrian.'

'Who is?'

'The Roman emperor.'

'Is he?'

'Well he was ... he's been dead years, Virago says.'

'He'll not want a lot to eat then.' Bella smiled and went off to grind some corn.

Walli took a deep breath and turned to face the north. The Wall seemed to watch as Walli passed underneath its arch, through the gate and into the chilly wind of the Pictland moor. It wasn't the wind that made him shiver. It wasn't the swampy soil oozing over his sandals.

It was the fear he might not return ... well, not alive anyway.

DAGGERS, DORMICE AND DROPPINGS

Walli trudged round the swampy moor trying to keep his feet out of the deeper puddles. A child on the hilltop was on lookout duty. She raced down into the Pict village crying, 'The Romans are attacking! The Romans are coming! The invasion has started!'

The warriors grabbed their weapons and gathered in the patch of grass in the middle of the village. 'How many?' Maggie McKilt demanded. 'A legion?'

'One,' the child said.

'One what?' the queen asked.

'One soldier. All on his own,' the child said.

Maggie rewarded the lookout with a firm slap around the ear. 'Idiot. That is not a Roman invasion.'

'I was only doing my job,' the child wailed and tears bubbled in her eyes.

Maggie ignored her and turned to the warriors. 'Best get back to your hut, you men. No need for a Roman spy to see the size of our fighting force.'

The men nodded and went off to hide. Maggie gathered the older women round her and they quickly helped one another to paint their faces. They stood, arms crossed, and prepared to face the Roman invader.

Walli trembled as he stepped into the clearing in the village and was faced with a scowling line of wild-haired women, each clutching a long dagger across a large chest.

Their faces were most terrible of all. They were smeared with blue paint.

As you know this is a sort of warpaint called 'woad'. The Picts were known to the Romans as the 'painted people' ... 'Pict – picture', get it? And the blue paint would make anyone look scary. Anyone except Maggie McKilt ... she looked scarier than a bear with red hair even without the woad. But the woad put them in the mood to fight. You could say it was the first-ever case of woad rage.

'Good afternoon,' Walli said with a weak smile. 'Greetings from Captain Obnoctius and the Roman legions!'

Maggie hardly moved. 'Tell Obnoctius to stick his Roman greetings up his Roman nose or we'll come over the Wall and do it for him.'

'That's nice,' the soldier said and tried to smile.

'You Romans aren't happy with invading us...'

'I'm a Gaul...'

'...You Romans, you're not happy with taking our men away.'

'... from Gaul...'

'... but you Romans now let your British friends snatch our children...'

'He was on the wrong side of the Wall.' Walli shrugged.

At last Maggie moved. She snatched at the scarf around Walli's neck and pulled it so tight he began to choke. 'Wrong answer, little man. It's you who are on the wrong side of the Wall. If the British witches can hold my Don to ransom then we can hold you to ransom.' She turned and looked at the women behind her. 'What do you say? A straight swap ... this Roman soldier for my Don?'

'No-o!' Jinny laughed. 'Ask for your Don back and weapons and food!'

The other women shouted their demands. 'Wine!' 'Eggs!' 'A nice woollen blanket for my bed.'

'No!' Walli cried through his choking throat. 'They won't give you anything!'

'Hah!' Maggie roared. 'Then they can have you back one piece at a time. First we'll cut off your fingers and then an arm, a leg and then your head. Then they'll see what happens to kidnappers.'

She placed her knife against his scrawny throat and he gasped, 'I'm a dead man ... I've been sentenced to be stoned to death anyway... They won't care if you kill me ... you'll just be saving them a pile of stones and a lot of mopping up blood ... and digging my grave ... you're choking me ... urk!'

Maggie McKilt let go of the soldier's scarf and he fell to the turf, panting. 'So, if you're not here to attack us, why are you here?'

'Message ... we have a visit from Emperor Hadrian...'

'He's dead.'

'That sort of thing doesn't stop the Romans,' Walli moaned as he rubbed his throat. 'Obnoctius wants to put on a Roman feast and some Roman games ... your tribe is invited.'

'Why?'

Walli shrugged. 'To make for a bigger crowd and to show how the Romans have tamed you...'

'What?' Maggie cried. 'Tamed us? I don't think so, little man.' She placed the tip of her dagger against his windpipe as he knelt on the ground in front of her.

Walli closed his eyes and spoke quickly. After all, these could be his last words and he wanted to get them right. 'The Romans know they can never defeat you ... that's why they built the Wall. But the Emperor will want to see just how mighty the Pict women are ... how dangerous in battle. Obnoctius wants you to come and fight like a gladiator.'

Maggie lowered the knife. 'Fight? Fight who?'

'Queen Virago.'

Maggie's blue face split in a big grin and she started to strut in front of the line of women. 'Not much of a fight – I will slice her like a sacrificial goat with the first stroke of my sword, won't I, my clan folk?'

The women gave a bit of a feeble cheer.

Maggie turned back to him. 'And when I win? Do I get my little Don back?'

Walli winced. 'The Captain doesn't know the boy is your son … he plans to put him in the catapult and fire him at the Wall … but if you win you have the right to fire the catapult. That's when you can kill the boy or spare him.'

Maggie thought about it for a while. 'I have to fight for my son's life and for my own life?'

'You could say that.'

'The Romans will let us return to Pictland if I win?' she asked.

'You return, with the boy,' Walli nodded.

'But not that ball thing,' Jinny called out. 'Please don't let him come back with the ball!'

Maggie glared at her and they stood blue face to blue face for a few angry moments. 'Jinny McGargle, you are as sour as ten-week old milk. And that woad makes you look like a bluebottle. Now hold your vicious tongue and get back to your weaving – I want a new battle kilt – finest wool you've got. One that leaves my arms free but hides a piece of Roman armour I'll use to cover my chest.'

'It'll need to be a big bit of armour to cover that chest,' Jinny muttered as she turned away and went to her cottage.

'Where will you get Roman armour?' Walli asked.

'None of your business,' the Pict queen snapped. 'And

if you tell your friends on the wrong side of the Wall about my armour, I will slit your throat from ear to ear.'

'Where to where?' Walli wondered.

'No … not here to here … ear to ear. Now get back and say the Picts will take up the challenge. We will see you tomorrow for the greatest battle Hadrian and his Wall have ever seen!'

Walli nodded and scurried away. His weak legs carried him through the softest, splashiest part of the swamp and he didn't mind. He just wanted to get away from that worrying woman.

***

Arturo sat in the midst of the British women and took a small book from a pocket in his tunic. 'It's written down here … just how cruel the Romans are! Listen, I'll read it to you…' he said and began to read slowly.

No, he wasn't a slow reader. He was reading it in the Roman language, Latin. Then he was turning it into the British language in his head before speaking. And the British women thought Arturo was ever so clever … and not bad looking either.

'The history writer, Suetonius is describing the execution of Emperor Vitellius over two hundred years ago. Listen … The soldiers tied his arms behind his back, put a noose around his neck and dragged him in his torn clothes to the Forum. All along the way the crowds greeted him with cruel shouts. His head was held back by the hair as they did with common criminals. They pelted him with dogs' droppings. At the Forum he was tortured for a long time, then killed. His body was dragged off with a hook and thrown into the River Tiber.'

'Awful!' old Bella sighed.

'Cruel,' the other women agreed.

'Great!' Dandelion smiled. 'That's what I'd like to do to that Pict boy. I like the bit where they pelt him with dogs' droppings. Maybe I'll do that before we fire him at the Wall.'

'Only if your Ma wins the fight,' Bella reminded her.

'There is no way my Ma can lose to a ragged, fat sow like Maggie McKilt,' Dandelion jeered. 'In fact she could fight five Maggies at once and still win. It won't be a gladiator fight it'll be a simple slaying. You'll see.'

'We'll see,' Bella muttered.

***

In the palace of Queen Virago, Obnoctius was reading a book too.

When I say 'palace' I mean that's what Virago called it. In fact it was just a hut a bit bigger than the rest. It wasn't like the Roman mansions with stone walls, hot and cold baths and heated floors. In fact it didn't have any baths at all – hot or cold. That could be why Virago smelled like a wild boar's bed.

It was a history of Roman feasts. Virago and her closest

friends looked at him blankly.

'Where will we get camel heels?' the queen asked quietly.

Obnoctius looked down his nose at her and twisted his mouth in what was supposed to be scorn … in fact he looked like he was chewing a thistle.

'My good woman, you get camel heels from camels! In fact you can get four camel heels from a single camel,' he added with a smirk.

Virago nodded. 'Fine. So where will we get camels?'

'What?'

'Where will we get the camels to get camel heels?' she asked.

'Ah ... yes ... well ... there are a lot of camels in North Africa but I suppose it's a little late to bring them to Britain now. Of course camels are used like horses in the deserts ... I suppose you could use horse heels!'

Virago sighed. 'We need the horses to pull the ploughs, take our carts to market and ride into battle if we have to. Horses with no heels are no use to us.'

I suppose not,' Obnoctius said. 'Let's see what else the book says about emperor feasts. One man called Trimalchio roasted a wild boar and when they cut it open a flock of song-thrushes flew out. Could you manage that?'

'Not a lot of song thrushes up here,' Bella said. 'We could catch a few sparrows maybe?'

Obnoctius shook his head angrily. 'Dormice ... Roman emperors love dormice roasted and stuffed with sausage meat.'

'Dormice? No. We have a few rats in the grain store,' one of the women said.

The Roman Captain jabbed a finger at the book, 'Snails ... lots of snails. Put them in a dish of blood to fatten them up then boil them and serve them.'

'We can do snails,' Virago said with a graceful bow of the head. 'Lots of them crawling around the fields. Mind you, they grow fat feasting on sheep droppings ... is that as good as fresh blood?'

'I don't think you are trying very hard to please our

noble Emperor,' Obnoctius said sourly. 'Look ... here are the birds they like to eat ... crows? Gulls? Jackdaws? Ravens? Peacocks? Coots? Swans?'

'It's catching them's the problem,' Bella said. 'We can offer him some mutton ... sheep are easier to catch.'

'Anyone can eat mutton,' Obnoctius cried. 'This is an emperor ... look, Elagabalus served his guests six hundred ostrich tongues ... that's the sort of thing I'm looking for. Parrot heads by the dozen? Flamingo brains by the hundred?'

'Fine,' Virago said, standing up. 'Leave it with us, you cuddly little Roman and we will come up with all of those.'

'Will we?' Bella asked.

Virago gave her a secret wink. 'Of course we will. You'd better be getting back to your little fort before it gets dark,' she warned Obnoctius. 'Unless you'd care to share my cosy bed in this palace?'

The Roman looked at the fleeces jumping with fleas and decided it was best to go.

... to flee, in fact! Ha! Ha! Laugh? I thought you'd never start.

'I'll be back tomorrow with some sauces from the fort. We have a very tasty one made from the rotten guts of fish. Delicious,' he said as he walked quickly back to the milecastle.

Walli was just entering the gate, very muddy and

weary. 'Well?' the Captain asked.

'Well … the Picts agreed to come to the games tomorrow,' Walli told him.

'You did well,' Obnoctius said. 'Of course if anything goes wrong the Emperor will enjoy watching us stone you to death,' he added as he walked up the steps to the Wall and headed home.

'But if nothing goes wrong I'm safe?' Walli called after him.

The Captain stopped and looked back. 'Don't be foolish. Your other task is to find the lost troop. But I am kind. I will give you until noon tomorrow. Fail with that and you die anyway! I haven't forgotten, you know. I'm not a fool!' he squawked. 'Do I look like a fool?'

But he turned away before Walli could answer that tricky question. The trumpeter ran from the tower where he'd been dozing and tried to keep in step with his captain. 'Par-parp-a-parp-parp! Par-parp-a-phuttttt!'

CHRISTIANS, CRIMINALS AND CANNIBALS

Walli sat gloomily in the dim room at the top of the tower as the sun set over the western hills. 'Could be my last sunset,' he moaned. 'I could be dead by this time tomorrow – if the Captain doesn't kill me the Picts probably will.'

'Hah! The Captain won't kill you!' Arturo laughed.

'He won't?'

'No! He'll get the troop to kill you. He'll get us to put you up against the Wall and stone you to death. You gathered a fine pile of stones this morning. They will come in very handy.'

Walli felt tears fill his eyes. 'You wouldn't throw any of the stones though, would you, Arturo? You wouldn't hurt your old comrade?'

Arturo wrapped an arm around his friend's shoulder. 'Of course I would! I'd pick a really big stone and crush your skull – it would kill you before you know it. I wouldn't want to see you suffer.'

'Thanks,' Walli said.

'In fact one minute you'll be standing there and the next you'll wake up on the shores of Ugliness.'

'Where?'

'The Roman afterlife.'

'But we're Gauls … we don't believe in the Roman

gods, do we?'

Arturo held up his book to the oil lamp. 'But the Roman ideas sound ... they sound right. There is this story about a man who went to the underworld and saw the unburied dead scattered around.'

'Is it true?'

'It must be ... it's in a book,' Arturo told him and patted one of the books he kept in his pack.

'In this afterlife there are "Furies" – women with wings that take revenge on you after you're dead!'

'On me?'

'On anyone that dies a violent death,' Arturo said.

'That's not me,' Walli trembled.

'Not now it's not ... but it will be if we stone you to death tomorrow.'

'Ah! What will happen to me in the underworld?' Walli asked.

'Says here ... look ... "On the shores of Ugliness there was a huge plain, covered with corpses that had suffered dreadful deaths. Some had been beheaded and some crucified. Pitiful bodies stood there with their throats freshly cut. The Furies were laughing at the misery of the victims. There was a sickening smell of blood." See?'
Walli nodded and swallowed hard to stop himself from being sick. 'Want some cheese?' Arturo asked.

'No ... I'm not hungry.'

'And of course you won't want to go to sleep,' Arturo told him. 'You'd just have nightmares about the Furies picking over your corpse, wouldn't you?'

'Would I?'

'Probably. So that's why it's better you stay awake ...
enjoy your last night on earth...'

'My last night?'

'Just in case,' Arturo said and hugged his comrade. 'It
would be a waste to spend it asleep. Tell you what ... as
you are my very best friend ... I will do you a favour.'

'What's that?'

'I will let you do my guard duty tonight. I'll sleep ...
and take the risk of getting nightmares ... while you can
stay awake on watch. Make sure those Picts don't try to
sneak across and rescue the boy.'

Walli opened his mouth but Arturo went on. 'No ... no
... no ... no need to thank me. I'll be just lying here if you
need me. If the women try to sneak up and cut your
throat just cry out and I'll be right by your side ... as soon
as I've dressed, had a wash and combed my hair.'

'Thanks,' Walli said. 'You make me feel much better.'
In fact I could manage a bit of that bread and cheese
now.'

'Sorry, mate. All gone. You should have eaten it when
you had the chance. I'd have saved you some.'

'Thanks.'

'Well?' Arturo said and nodded to the tower door. 'Off
you go ... and close the door on your way out. Don't want
a draft to disturb my hair, do we?'

'No.'

'Night-night!'

Walli wandered out into the chill night air and stared
over towards Pictland. Not even a fire there tonight to
light the darkness. Clouds hid the moon and stars.

It must have been on a night like this, he decided, when the Picts attacked the lost legion. Dragged them off the Wall to their deaths. Cut their throats and left them to lie on the shores of Ugliness with their heads hanging off.

His eyes felt heavy. It had been a hard day.

Walli squatted down in the shelter of the parapet and closed his eyes. As he began to doze the maze in his mind began to untangle. 'That's what must have happened to the lost legion,' he sighed. 'If I tell Obnoctius I've solved the secret he'll spare my life!' He smiled in the darkness and did what he did best.

He fell asleep. And in his dreams he dreamed about the lost troop. They were laughing and happy. They weren't on the shores of Ugliness! In his dreams he saw where they really were. The real secret. And Walli had it. He was safe.

But by morning he'd forgotten the dream – forgotten he ever knew the secret.

***

A few brave birds sat on the Wall and sang their dawn songs. Walli woke. He looked over the parapet and for once the cold Pictish wind didn't blast his face. The wind was soft and mild and blew from the south. Nice weather for a picnic. 'A good day for a feast,' he said to himself. 'A good day to die, probably.'

He looked north and saw Maggie McKilt striding over the hill from the Pictish village at the head of her tribe of women and children. The warrior men had been left behind. She was dressed in a short kilt that showed her legs and arms – a tunic for fighting. Walli hoped the

Emperor wouldn't be too shocked by the sight. Two women behind the Queen carried her mighty sword. The Picts shared the same dark scowl.

To the east there was the clatter of hobnailed sandals getting closer as the troop from the fort marched towards the Milecastle.

To the south the Britons in the village were stirring and starting to lay out a feast on cloths. Children were set to guard the food from the dogs that trotted round, with dripping tongues and glittering eyes.

Virago looked at the wooden plates proudly and checked with Bella. 'Snails?'

'Well ... sheep tongues cut into a hundred little pieces – they look like ostrich tongues and probably taste of ostrich tongues. Who knows?'

'Flamingo brains?'

'Brains from that dead horse we found in a ditch last week. Boiled and cut up into little balls to look like flamingo brains. Not that I've ever seen a flamingo ... but it's a bird, isn't it? I mean it won't have a horse-sized brain or it wouldn't be able to fly!'

'Good thinking, Bella.'

'Dormice?'

'A couple of dozen, Virago.'

'Aren't they a bit big for dormice?'

'Well, when they were alive they were rats ... now they're dead they are dormice.'

'Fair enough. Stuffed with pork sausage?'

'Stuffed with horse sausage.'

'That'll do. No roast boar with song-birds stitched inside?'

'We sort of trimmed the horse ... well the bit that hadn't rotted away in the ditch ... and put a few live rats inside.'

'That'll be fun.' Virago chuckled.

'No ... the rats just ate their way out. I suppose we could pop one of the kids inside to leap out when it's cut open?'

'Hah!' Virago barked. 'Our kids would eat their way out quicker than the rats! No, just leave it. The Emperor will probably be too excited by the gladiator contest to worry about food. There's always that fresh bread, of course.'

'No, that's for Adrian.'

'Adrian? The monk? Lawd, I'd forgotten he was coming! He wants to preach to the whole village. Says he's bringing crispy vanity to the British people!'

'Not crispy vanity ... Christianity,' Bella said.

'I knew that,' Virago snorted. 'Anyway my sister says it's great – none of those messy sacrifices and the Romans taking all your best animals to slaughter for their gods. You get to eat bread and drink wine. Only one god, she says.'

'What's he called then?' Bella asked.

'Dunno ... just God, I think.'

'Much simpler than all those Jupiter and Juno, Mars and Venus you have to remember.'

'Much simpler.' Virago nodded. 'You wouldn't believe some of the gods the Romans have.' the Queen sighed.

'Last time I was at the fort they told me about Cordea ... goddess of door hinges!'

Yes, I know it sounds crazy. But it is true. Think about it – if a door hinge breaks then the door will fall and might crack you on the head and kill you. Really it would be useful to have a goddess of door hinges to stop that happening ... and they did. Honest.

'I don't believe it!'

'I said you wouldn't.' Virago chuckled. 'They have Penates ... spirits of cupboards, Robigus the god of mildew...'

'Of what?'

'That nasty mouldy fungus that grows in damp places.'

'I know what you mean.'

'Sabazius: god of weeds as far as I can see. And even Terminus … a god of boundaries.'

'Like the Wall?'

'Well the Wall has TWO gods because it has a god of doorways too – Janus!'

'Oh!' Bella moaned. 'The sooner we get this Christianity with just the one God the better.'

'Ah, but there's a catch,' Virago said.

'There always is,' Bella sighed.

'The Christians eat bread and wine at their services.'

'So you said.'

'Well, it seems they believe the bread turns into the flesh of their God's son, Jesus as they swallow it.'

'Really?'

'Really. And the wine turns into his blood.'

'They believe that?'

'They do. Well the Romans say if they're eating human flesh and drinking human blood they are cannibals,' Virago said in a low voice.

'They would.'

'So, whenever they get their hands on a Christian they execute them. They had one emperor – Nero – he stuck a hundred Christians on poles, covered them in tar and set fire to them. They lit up his palace gardens at night.'

'Ah, cruel people,' Bella said quietly.

'Of course usually, I mean usually, they just execute them.'

'So this Adrian monk feller…'

'…had better not turn up and start preaching while the

Romans are around!' Virago murmured. 'Anyway, we can't stand here all morning chatting about cannibals. We need to get the animal hunts ready.'

'They are called venatores,' Bella said smugly.

'I knew that,' Virago snapped. 'Here come the Romans,' she said, pointing along the Wall.

'This will be fun,' Bella said.

'Excuse me, Bella, but actually it will be no fun fighting that Maggie McKilt to the death,' Virago said.

Bella nudged her in the ribs. 'Oh, go on, you'll enjoy that. After you kill her you can stick her head on a pole – the Romans might even let you put it over the gateway so she can look out at Pictland.'

Virago gave a grim smile. 'I suppose you're right, Bella. I have to think of the Britons and how much pleasure that would give them.'

The two women walked arm-in-arm to greet the Roman legion.

***

Maggie and the Picts looked up and called to Walli, 'Are you going to open the gates then or do we have to climb the Wall?'

'I'll let you in,' he called and ran down the stairs to the gateway. The Pict women and children walked through carefully. Looking for a trap. But there was none.

Moments later the Roman legion, led by Obnoctius and his trumpeter reached the Milecastle and marched down. Obnoctius stood on the second step (to make himself look taller).

He called, 'Now you Picts, I want no trouble today. We are here to enjoy ourselves. See some blood spilled, eat flamingo tongues, execute some criminals and see at least one gladiator die. I want no violence, do I make myself clear?'

'Aye,' the women muttered.

'You Picts will stay near the Wall – you can climb to the top if you want a better view – but I don't want you mixing with the British and starting trouble. Ah, here comes our hostess, Queen Virago. Three cheers for Queen Virago! Hip, hip…'

Silence.

As the Picts arranged themselves on the Milecastle stairs Obnoctius crossed to the British Queen. 'So, my loyal ally, where is Emperor Hadrian?'

Virago frowned. 'Isn't he with you?' she asked.

Obnoctius shook his head. 'My guard, Walachia, told me you were preparing for Hadrian's visit.'

'No … we were preparing for the monk Adrian's visit … you were the one who said you were expecting Hadrian!'

Obnoctius's mouth opened and closed like a drowning trout. 'Ah … oh … there seems to have been some sort of mistake. Never mind, it is the last mistake that cowardly little Gaul will make. He can die with the other criminals.' He turned to Arturo who had just wandered down from the tower looking sleepy. 'You!'

'Yes, sir?'

'Lock that man in the tower. He dies at noon!' he said, pointing at a stunned Walli.

FEATHERS, FEASTING AND FLIGHT

The animal hunting went down very well. There were no lions, but there was Dandelion. She faced a flock of fierce sheep and had only one, small, shaggy dog to help.

The sheep glared at her and munched on the grass. They didn't want to move. Dandelion placed her fingers to her lips and whistled. The little dog sped round to the back of the sheep.

Another whistle and the dog lay down.

The sheep began to move. First they moved away from Dandelion and went between two posts that had been hammered into the soil.

Then more whistles sent the dog to turn the sheep around and make them trot towards a sheep pen with a gate.

One sheep with fierce, curled horns turned to face the dog. The dog lay still. Would the sheep charge away from the pen? It stamped its back foot and turned towards Dandelion, who held the gate open. Would it attack her and gore her?

A whistle. The dog edged forward. The sheep took fright and ran into the pen. The other sheep followed and Dandelion slammed the gate.

Even the Picts cheered at her skill. Dandelion bowed to the Picts on the Wall, to the Romans who sat on the grass of the vallum and then to the Britons who sat on the mound.

People are still doing this two thousand years later. It could make a television programme! But what would you call it? 'Who are ewe looking at?' 'Fleece circus'? 'Go back to sheep'? 'If ewe can't bleat 'em, join 'em'? Or the winner could get to eat the sheep at the end so let's call it 'Snack baa'. If you think any of these ideas are good then ewe should get out more.

Then it was the turn of the bullfighter. A sleepy bull was brought into a circle of fencing that had been put up overnight. The gate opened and one of the Roman soldiers from Spain entered. He took his sword in one hand and a red cloak in the other.

At first the bull ignored him so the soldier jabbed it in the rump with his sword. The bull turned and snorted. The Spanish soldier waved the cloak under its steaming nostrils and flicked it at its nose.

The bull lowered its head and walked towards him. The Spaniard let it push the cloak aside while he held it away from his body. He did this four or five times, each time letting the horns brush closer to his body. The Romans began to cheer. This seemed to upset the bull. It began to trot around the ring now and the Spaniard was sweating.

Suddenly the bull headed straight for him. The man turned and tried to run away but the bull caught his backside between its horns and lifted its head sharply. The Spaniard wailed as he flew through the air, clean over the fence and landed on the grass.

The bull put its head down and set off after him. The

fence was splintered like a winter twig as the bull broke into a gallop.

The Spaniard raised his sword but it had bent when he landed. The bull roared. The crowd roared and the soldier set off to run for the safety of the fort ... two miles away. Pounding hooves and bellows, screams and Spanish curses faded into the east.

The chicken hunt was more dangerous. Two British women, two Celts and two Romans had to chase and capture as many of the dozen chickens as they could. To make it interesting they each had a sack tied over their head.

The They crashed into one another and punched whoever stood in their way. When a chicken clucked they raced towards the sound. When a hawk flew over, the chickens rushed, crying, for the shelter of the Wall.

The hunters ran towards the sound. Some fell over chickens in a cloud of feathers, some fell over one another … and they all ended up crashing into the Wall.

Hoods were pulled off to show cracked skulls, bleeding noses and black eyes.

Obnoctius called, 'I declare the winners are …' He gave a long pause. '… the chickens!'

Obnoctius slapped his leg in joy and said to his centurion, 'Emperor Hadrian doesn't know what he's missing. He should have been here.'

The centurion gave him a curious look and said, 'Yes, sir.'

***

The crowd cheered.

The sun rose in the sky and Virago said, 'That ends the morning show, ladies and gentlemen … and Picts. Please join us at the feast.'

There was such a rush for the food the children guarding it were flattened and had to be rescued, sobbing. The Picts ate twice as much as the soldiers, whose armour didn't save them from the sharp elbows of the battling women.

When the last horse brain and sheep tongue had been scoffed, when the last roasted rat had been swallowed and the last horse sausage stuffed in a famished face, the women and the soldiers went back to their places.

Obnoctius stood on the frame of the catapult and told them, 'Now for the executions. First, let us get rid of that cowardly Walachia. Bring him down from the tower!'

Two soldiers went up the stairs to collect the prisoner while another pair planted a tall stake of wood in the ground beside the Wall. Obnoctius explained. 'The law of Rome is famous around the world. It is fair but it punishes those who dare to defy us. This man,' he said pointing to the miserable Gaul who was carried down the stairway, 'This man fell asleep when he should have been guarding the camp. But I, the noble Obnoctius, spared his miserable life. I gave him a chance.'

'You're a little hero,' Virago called and the British villagers clapped politely. 'A real little hero.'

'I am not little,' the Captain said, blushing. 'I gave this man a second chance. All he had to do was discover where the lost troop of Milecastle 13 had vanished to. Have you done that?'

The Pict women leaned forward from their place on the Wall to catch his answer. Walli wrinkled his forehead, 'Last night ... when I fell asleep ... I dreamed ... I had the answer.'

'And the answer is?'

'I don't remember ... I woke up.'

'Ahhhh!' the Pict women sighed.

'Tie him to the stake in the ground. Take that pile of stones. When I give the signal I want you to throw the stones at him till he is dead.'

The soldiers walked slowly over to the pile of stones and each picked one up. They stood in a line, facing the Wall and watched as Walli was tied to the post.

The women from both sides were silent. They hid their children's faces in their shawls. Killing in battle was one thing, but this was cruel and unfair.

When Walli's hands were tied Obnoctius moved to the end of the row. 'Trumpeter, sound the execution fanfare!'

The trumpeter gave a sad 'Pa-aa-arp! A-pa-aa-arp a-pa-aa-arp!'

A tear rolled down Walli's cheek. He was a brave man really and not afraid to die. 'I just wish I could have seen Teutoburger Forest once more before I died,' he whispered. He shook his head and let the tear fall on the foreign grass. He was ready. He looked the execution troop in the eye. One at a time he looked into their faces. One at a time they looked away.

'Take aim!' the captain cried. The soldiers raised their throwing arms. 'And fire!'

A shower of rocks whistled through the air. They smashed into the Wall and shattered into pieces. Obnoctius blinked. He rubbed his eyes. 'You missed!' he screamed. 'Every one of you missed! Try again, you Gaul goons and Spanish simpletons. Try again! Take aim! Fire!'

Whoosh! Crash! Splinter.

They missed again. The pile of stones was getting smaller now.

A small smile spread across Walli's lips. 'Teutoburger,' he murmured. 'I WILL see you again.'

'Again!' the officer raged.

And again they missed. Obnoctius picked up the last stone – which was not a very large one. He drew back his arm and threw it as hard as he could. The rock soared over Walli's head and made straight for Maggie McKilt where she sat on the top of the Wall. The Pict Queen ducked and glared at the Roman.

'Sorry,' Obnoctius shrugged. He turned to the troop. 'Very well, if we can't throw a stone at this man we will throw the man at the stone. Put him in the catapult, aim it at the Wall – but not at Queen Maggie – and fire.'

Walli was untied and taken to the catapult. Arturo wound the catapult arm back and led Walli to the bowl on the end. Suddenly Dandelion ran forward. 'Captain Obnoctius,' she cried. 'The man will get cold if he rushes through the air. He could die of the cold.'

'So?'

'So … let me wrap him in this cloak before he is fired,' she begged.

Virago wasn't sure what her daughter was up to but she stepped behind her to help. 'You can't stop a man having a last request before he dies, cuddly little Captain, can you?'

'Can't I?'

'It's not the British way,' she told him.

'Oh, very well. But be quick. We have the boy to deal with next and then the gladiators.'

Dandelion took a large, square woollen cloak. She didn't fasten it around Walli's neck but tied the top corners to each of his wrists instead. Then she tied the bottom corners to his ankles. She reached up to whisper in his ear, 'When the catapult fires, spread your arms.'

Walli gave a small nod to show he'd heard, then let Arturo place him in the bowl.

'Goodbye, my oldest and dearest friend,' the tall Gaul said. 'I won't cry when you die – but I will miss you.'

'You're very brave,' Walli said. 'But don't worry. I'm not going to die. We'll see Teutoburger again. Together. We will!'

Arturo patted his comrade on the shoulder and released the catapult. The rush of wind made Walli gasp. When the arm of the catapult reached to the top it crashed to a halt but the soldier flew on. He saw the top of the Wall waiting to smash every bone he owned plus a lot of brain and guts. Then he remembered the girl's words. He spread his arms and legs as wide as he could.

The great square of the cloak opened like the wings of a bat and lifted him up. His belly grazed the top of the Wall and he was flying over the Pictish marsh towards the hill.

A dandelion seed in the wind drifts down softly when its 'umbrella' catches the wind. The cloak was like an umbrella and it slowed Walli's fall. A fall to earth would still have shattered his ankles but he was heading for the soft peat of the marshes.

His heels struck hard and he sank in the swampy ground up to his knees. He was stuck fast – but alive and unhurt. He flapped at the cloak and struggled to free himself. But he'd landed in the softest part of the marsh. The more he struggled the more he sank.

He'd been saved from the brutal quick death of a Wall smash only to face the gentle but slow terror of drowning.

'Don't struggle,' a man's voice said.

Walli twisted round. He saw the group of Pictish warriors who had come from the village. They stood around the edge of the swamp and looked at him. They carried large oblong shields – each almost as tall as a man. 'You stole your shields from the Romans!' Walli shouted. 'The lost troop! You massacred them and stole their weapons! That's what happened to them! Now you're going to kill me.' Walli thrashed around in a panic when he realized the danger. 'You're the Attacotti … you want to drag me out so you can cook me and eat me!'

It just got worse, he decided. Saved from smashing into the Wall, saved from drowning … now nothing could save him from being roasted alive and eaten!

The warriors laughed. They placed their shields in the swamp, edge to edge, to make a pathway across to him. The mud was almost up to his armpits now. The leader of the warriors managed to slip a rope under Walli's arms and tie it in a noose.

The ten men from the village each gripped the rope and pulled. Slowly Walli was dragged free of the sucking slime. He slithered on to the path of shields and was soon squirming at the feet of the men who had rescued him.

He looked up and they laughed happily. 'You're laughing because I'm your supper, aren't you?'

'No,' one man smiled. 'We're laughing because the swamp has sucked off your trousers!'

Walli looked down. 'Oh,' he said and tried to pull down his tunic.

'Never mind, we have more in the village,' the leader said. 'Good Roman Army trousers.

'From the men you massacred?' Walli groaned.

'No, from the Roman Army. They gave them to us when they forced us to join the army in Gaul. We dumped them when we escaped and joined our friends the Picts.'

'Escaped?' Walli said, wondering. And then he remembered the dream. 'Of course! The lost troop! You didn't disappear ... you deserted ... you ran off to Pictland!. You're the lost troop!'

'The leader nodded. 'We are. Want to join us?'

'And live in this awful place?' he asked.

'One day we'll cross back into Britannia, then find our way back home. Do you have a home you want to return to? If you do, we can help you.'

Arturo always said that big Gauls don't cry. But Walli wept as he said, 'Oh, yes. Thank you … oh, yes! My Teutoburger – I want to see my Teutoburger Wald again!'

GLADIATORS, GOATSKINS AND GODS

Obnoctius was an angry man. 'I wanted that soldier executed. I wanted to show my troops what happens to soldiers who fall asleep at their post!' He was spluttering so much the spittle almost drowned a hedgehog that scuttled along by the Wall. 'I wanted everyone to see what happens to a man who fails to obey an order from Obnoctius Minimus! I wanted ... I wanted to see him dying ... not flying! The next execution WILL work, even if I have to use my own sword to send the villain to Hades! Who is it?'

'The boy, Captain,' Virago said.

Obnoctius strutted over to the catapult and ordered Arturo to wind it back. 'Fetch the boy,' he demanded.

Don McKilt looked up when the curtain over the doorway opened and the weasel-faced British girl peered in. 'Your turn, pathetic Pict,' she said and untied him from the post he was tied to.

'I'll gut you and use your bladder to make a ball-foot,' he hissed.

'Yeah? A boy in a dress threatens me? Ooooh-er! I'm so scared. Gut me? You and whose army?' she jeered.

'We have an army,' he said. 'They'll rescue me and then I'll skin you alive – one strip at a time. Then I'll cut off your head and nail it over the door of our hut just the way the old Celts did.'

'Oh yeah?'

'Yeah.'

'Oh ye-e-e-a-a-ahhh?'

'Ye-e-e-a-a-ahhh!'

'Oh reeeeally?'

'Yes!'

'Dandelion, what are you doing in there? Cutting him free or cuddling him?' Virago's voice screeched.

Dandelion blushed and pulled the rope free. 'I'd rather cuddle a cow,' she sniffed.

'I'd rather cuddle a cowpat.'

The Picts on the Wall went silent as they watched Don McKilt being led from the village, over the mound and towards the catapult. Don McKilt grinned up at Maggie. 'You've come to rescue me,' he said. 'I knew you would.'

Maggie walked down the steps from the Wall and crossed to the Roman Captain. 'I want to fight for the life of the boy,' she said.

'We agreed that, Queen Maggie, and a Roman always keeps his word.'

'It's time for the gladiator show, isn't it?' Maggie said.

Obnoctius looked up to the sun which was past the midday mark. 'It is.'

'And a gladiator can claim rewards, can't they?'

'Sometimes.'

'Then I want to fight Queen Virago. If I win then the boy goes free ... I claim his life as my prize,' she explained.

He scowled. 'Somebody has to die today,' he moaned.

'That's what the games are all about. Death and bloodshed. It's what our gods want to see. We spill blood as a sacrifice to the gods.'

Maggie McKilt gave a grim smile. 'If I win the contest then you will see Queen Virago's blood spilt … if I lose you will see my blood, then do what you wish with the boy.'

'Thanks, Ma,' Don said bitterly.

'Well, you wouldn't want to go on living alone if I was dead, would you?' she asked.

'He might!' Dandelion argued.

'Whose side are you on?' Virago raged.

'Sorry, Ma,' Dandelion muttered miserably. All this killing seemed exciting … until it suddenly seemed real and rather rotten.

Suddenly Don understood. 'If my Ma kills your Ma I'll make sure no harm comes to you,' he promised.

'And I'll do my best to save you,' the girl muttered.

Both children blinked back tears and tried to hide them.

'Agreed.' Obnoctius nodded, pleased that someone would be sure to die today after all. Don McKilt was placed in the bowl of the catapult, ready to be fired at the Wall if his mother lost.

Virago used her sword to slash away the bottom half of her skirts so her legs were as free to move as Maggie's were in her short kilt. Each woman picked up a shield.

Obnoctius sat on the frame of the catapult, next to Arturo, and clapped, excitedly. 'We who are about to die salute you.'

'What?' Virago and Maggie asked.

'It's what a group of gladiators said to an emperor once.

'We who are about to die salute you.'

They said that because they HOPED the Emperor, Claudius, would spare their lives. It didn't work and they died. Don't try it when you are sent to play hockey against a Glasgow Girls' school. You'll die once those modern Picts pick on you...

'Oh, all right,' Maggie sniffed.

'If you say so,' Virago sighed. She picked up a small shield and let it cover her left arm. 'Now can I get on with killing her?'

'This is good,' Obnoctius laughed. 'Even in Rome it's rare to see women gladiators. They're a bit of a laugh ... like clowns or Andabatae.'

Arturo pulled a book form his tunic and said, 'Juvenal wrote a poem about them, sir.'

'About women gladiators?'

'Yes, sir.'

'Then read it ... let it be part of the games!' Obnoctius said. He cleared his throat. 'Silence while I recite the poet Juvenal!'

Arturo stood on the lowest step of the Wall and began to recite:

'See how she slashes at dummies of wood
As she trains for the fighting, she is simply no good.

See how the helmet just weighs down her head
Though there's really no chance that she'll end up plain dead.

Why does she fight? Does she think she's a bloke?
Her husband should tell her she looks like a joke.

The bandages thick make her legs look like trees,
We laugh when she rests as she squats down and pees.

Panting and groaning with sweat on her face,
She only brings women pure shame and disgrace.'

The Roman soldiers clapped loudly. The women of the British and Pict tribes just glared at him.

At last the women faced one another. 'My gods, look at your face, Queen Virago,' Maggie McKilt sneered.

'Was anyone else hurt in the accident?'

'You won't upset me, even if you talk till you're blue in the face … ooooh! I say … you are blue in the face. Suits you, dear.'

Maggie leapt at her but the Brigante Queen blocked the sword blow with her own sword and held it. Their noses were a finger-width apart. 'Your face is a mess,' Virago hissed. 'Don't you have a mirror in your kennel?'

She pushed the Pict away and they began to circle and jab at one another. 'I bet your mother had a loud bark,' Virago shouted.

'You should be kind to animals,' Maggie jeered. 'Why don't you give that monkey its face back. That blue face doesn't suit you, sweetie.' She smiled. 'It doesn't go with your red eyes.'

Virago flew at the Pict queen and Maggie beat aside the sword with her shield.

DANG!

She jumped forward and sliced at Virago. But as she stretched she slipped and fell to one knee.

Virago stepped forward and smacked at Maggie's ribs with the flat of her sword. There was a 'clang' and Virago's sword snapped.

'You cheat!' the British Queen roared. 'Wearing armour's cheating!'

Maggie McKilt laughed. 'No it's not. Romans wear it all the time, isn't that right, Captain?'

Obnoctius nodded. Maggie stepped forward and stabbed at Virago who could only push the sword away with her shield. Maggie jabbed quickly and the wood and leather of the shield began to split.

'Kill her!' the Pict women cried. Dandelion clung to Don and shuddered.

'Cheat!' the British women called but there was nothing they could do. Their Queen was about to be defeated.

'Surrender!' Dandelion screamed. 'Surrender, Ma. Let her have the brat back.'

'A Briton doesn't surrender,' Virago said and picked up a stone from the ground and flung it at Maggie. It hit the Pict woman with a clang but she kept moving forward. Virago stepped back and stepped into a slimy cowpat. She slipped and fell backwards. Her shield hit the ground and shattered. She had only the stump of a sword to defend herself.

'That'll make you smell a bit sweeter,' Maggie laughed as she raised her sword over her head.

'Beg for mercy, Ma!' Dandelion wailed.

Virago turned to her, furious. 'What have I always

taught you, Dandelion? Britons never beg ... and big girls don't cry. What did I say?'

'Big girls don't cry, Ma,' she moaned and scrubbed the tear tracks from her cheeks. Maggie McKilt grinned. Virago closed her eyes.

Everyone held their breath. In the silence one strange man's voice roared over the turf. 'Thou shalt not kill!'

The man stood on the mound. He was dressed in a tunic, trousers and cloak all sewn together from goatskins. His white hair fell to his waist and his beard was nearly as long. Virago scrambled to her feet, then fell straight on to her knees. 'Adrian! Father Adrian. Welcome to the North Brigantes.'

Maggie McKilt lowered her sword. Obnoctius jumped down from the catapult and walked across to her. 'Who is this ragged slave?' he asked crossly.

'It's Adrian. We've been waiting for him for weeks. He's come to preach … I mean speak to us.'

The Brigante women and children all fell to their knees. Even the Roman soldiers wandered across to look at the stranger.

Adrian stood glaring at them. 'What is this heathen Roman sport you are playing?' he demanded.

'Sorry, Father,' Virago said. 'The Romans are our masters. We have to do what they say.'

'You must do what God says,' the fierce old man said.

'Yes … well … him as well.' Virago shrugged. 'But the Romans are here … and God isn't.'

'Hah!' the man snorted. 'God is everywhere. Obey him first.'

Obnoctius strode over to the man and climbed to the top of the mound. 'Who do you think you are? You can't tell these people to disobey me.'

'I just did, shorty,' the monk said.

'What sort of priest are you? A priest of Jupiter? Does the Emperor know you are going around telling Britons to rebel?'

'I am a Christian, you stupid little man. Now get out of my way. I want to preach to these good people.'

Obnoctius stepped back and a wide grin split his face. 'Wonderful, oh, wonderful!' he cried. 'A Christian. I have always wanted to meet a Christian.'

'Then kneel with the others on the grass and listen.

Even you can be saved,' the old man promised.

'No, no, no!' Obnoctius cried and was hopping from one foot to the other. 'I mean I always wanted to meet a Christian so I could execute him.'

Me? Execute me?' Adrian said. 'Why would you want to do that?'

'We know all about you Christians. You're cannibals. You eat human flesh and drink blood…'

'Yes, but…'

'Arrest this man!' the Captain cried and about six soldiers rushed forward to grab him. Obnoctius waved them back. 'Two of you will do. The rest I want to find some wood and set up a stake. We'll tie him to it and leave him to die of hunger and thirst. After we've executed the Pict boy…'

Arturo edged close to Obnoctius. 'Sorry, sir, but the Picts have gone.'

'Gone? Gone where?'

'Home, sir.'

And it was true. While everyone had been looking south towards the mound and the monk, the Picts has quietly slipped Don McKilt away from his guard, Dandelion, and melted away through the open gate in the Milecastle.

Obnoctius cursed a Roman curse then sighed. 'Never mind, we have a more important execution to carry out. This will get me carried in triumph through the streets of Rome. This will make me famous! The generals are all jealous of me, you know. They know I am too clever for them. They think I will rule Rome if I do great deeds there. They sent me to this putrid Pict border to get me as far from Rome as possible.'

'Really?' Arturo said. 'I thought they sent you here so you could do no harm – to sort of get you out of the way?'

'Nonsense,' Obnoctius said. 'They're afraid of me. But after I've sent them the head of this Christian they will see what a truly great Roman I am.'

'He's just a crazy old man,' Arturo said.

'He's a blood-drinking cannibal,' the captain spat.

'Want me to leave you alone with him and a knife for an hour? Eh? Do you want that?'

'No, sir.'

'No, sir. Because we'd come back to find you drained like an empty wineskin. Drained, do you hear me?'

A soldier hurried up to Obnoctius. 'The stake is ready.'

He pointed to the Wall. A tall pole was propped against it.

'Right, men. Time to show these British peasants what we do to Christians. This will stop their silly prayers. To the Wall!'

'To the Wall!' the Romans cheered and they dragged the old man across the turf.

'Nonsense,' Obnoctius said.

'No, true as I'm standing here ... well, not exactly standing here. But true as I'm being dragged along here. Everyone in Rome's a Christian these days. Didn't they tell you? I suppose you're a bit out of touch ... being sent all the way up here.'

'I will return in triumph to Rome,' Obnoctius snapped.

'You'll return to Rome in chains if you execute me, I'm telling you,' Adrian argued.

The little Roman turned to his men. 'Now tie him to the top of the stake, and watch him suffer.'

Arturo and the soldiers looked up at the stake. 'How?'

'How what?'

'How do we get him up there?'

'Well ...' Obnoctius said, 'Well ... it's obvious.'

Is it?'

Yes.'

'Carry him up on a ladder, I suppose?' the tall Gaul asked.

'Obvious.'

'We don't have a ladder.'

'Then try something else,' Obnoctius exploded.

'What?'

What, what?'

'What should we try? We could haul him up on a rope but how do we tie him once he's up there?'

A Spanish soldier suggested, 'We could lower him down from the Wall.'

'Good thinking,' Obnoctius agreed.

'But we still can't bind him to the stake,' Arturo said.

'What we need,' Obnoctius said. 'What we need is ... a cup of wine. I think better after a cup of wine.'

I thought you said it was 'obvious',' Arturo told him.

'And I thought I told you I'd have you stoned to death for running away during a battle,' the Captain said nastily.

'Mock battle.'

'Real stones,' Obnoctius hissed. 'Now fetch me my wine!'

LOVE, LEGIONS
AND LIGHTNING

The sun was quite low in the sky by the time Obnoctius had finished a wineskin full of wine.

The old monk sat happily on the turf looking at the stake and the puzzled soldiers. At last he spoke. 'It's obvious,' he said.

'Yes,' Arturo sighed. 'So the Captain keeps telling us. But we can't see how to get you up on the stake.'

'Then I'll have to tell you how they do it.' The monk chuckled.

'Go on then.'

'You take the stake down,' he began.

'Take the stake down?' Obnoctius frowned.

'Lie the stake on the grass.'

'Lie it on the grass.'

'Fasten the victim to the stake.'

'Fasten the victim to the stake.'

'Then stand the stake up!'

The Captain's face was as red as the wine. 'Obvious, see?' he laughed. 'Obvious. I told you it was obvious. But you Gauls and Spanish were too stupid to see it, weren't you? It took a Roman brain to work it out. That's why we rule the world. Not with the power of our armies but with the power of our brains. See?'

'Yes, sir,' Arturo muttered.

'So what are you waiting for? Crucify the monk!'

'No wait!' Father Adrian squeaked. 'I'm afraid of heights. I get giddy if I stand on a molehill. Hoist me up there and it could kill me!'

'That's the idea,' Obnoctius said. 'But hoist you up there and you'll be well away from our noses. I don't mean to offend you, but you smell like a dead goat.'

'It's the skins. I'll change. I'll pop down into the valley and have a wash in the River Tyne,' he promised.

The soldiers were struggling with the massive stake but at last laid it on the grass. The monk was dragged over to it and his wrists and ankles bound and tied behind the pole with leather strands. It was even more difficult to raise up once the monk was fastened to it. It lay against the Wall and swayed in the breeze.

'I feel sick!' the old man moaned.

Obnoctius looked up … sadly just as the monk threw up. His last meal splattered on to the Captain's face and uniform.

'Oh, look what you've done, you careless old fool. I'll have to get back to the baths at the fort!'

'I could do with a nice warm bath myself,' the monk moaned. 'Let me down and I'll join you, eh?'

But Obnoctius had started to climb the stairs to the top of the Wall. Suddenly Dandelion raced after him. 'You're evil,' she screamed. 'That old bloke never did you any harm. God will be avenged.'

Obnoctius reached out a hand and grabbed her by the shoulder of her tunic.

Suddenly he pushed the girl to a Spanish soldier. 'Bring the girl with us to the camp.' He climbed the last steps to the top of the Wall and shouted to the Britons. 'Do not try to set the old man free,' he warned. 'If you do then I will make sure the little girl takes his place. Would you like that, Virago?'

The British Queen glared at him but shook her head.

The Romans formed into two lines and marched east after Obnoctius and his trumpeter. Only Arturo was left to guard the Milecastle and the monk.

'Defeated again,' Virago said bitterly.

'We could fight them,' Bella said fiercely. 'You're not going to let them get away with it, are you?'

Virago shook her head. 'Our men couldn't beat them. Even the painted Picts couldn't beat them. No one can beat them!'

'That is not true,' Arturo said. He was sitting on the top step enjoying the late afternoon sun. 'The Roman Army can be beaten,' he said.

'Yes, by Hannibal and an army of elephants,' Virago

sneered. 'We've all heard that old story. Where will we get elephants from?'

'No, by a tribe of Gauls,' Arturo said and tapped the book in his hand. 'It was a famous defeat almost three hundred years ago. The battle of Teutoburger Wald.'

'Wald?'

'Forest, then,' Arturo explained. 'The Romans lost the battle because they didn't believe they could lose. And they lost because they trusted the tribes they'd beaten.'

'Tribes like us?' old Bella asked.

'Tribes a bit like you,' the soldier said.

'See?' the old woman said, nudging Virago. 'If the Gauls can beat them then so can we.'

Virago sighed. 'We don't know how they did it, do we? And a Roman like him isn't going to tell us.'

'I'm a Gaul,' Arturo said.

Bella had a cunning look on her face. 'I don't suppose the Gaul could tell us anyway. He carries books around with him. But I don't think he can read them.'

'He read that gladiator poem,' Virago reminded her.

'Nah, he probably just learnt that from memory. If you asked him to read that story about that forest I bet he couldn't.'

Suddenly Virago caught on. 'You're right, Bella. He's just showing off. Same as all men.'

'No I'm not,' Arturo. 'I have the book inside the tower. I'll go and get it now,' he said walking across to the door. 'I'm actually a little hurt that you could think that.'

'Not as hurt as I am stuck up on this stake,' Adrian groaned as Arturo disappeared. 'If you don't get me down soon, Virago, I'll be dead by this time tomorrow.'

'Can't help,' the Queen shrugged. 'If it's between you and my daughter I'll save my daughter every time.'

'I know,' Adrian sighed. 'Can't say I blame you. I forgive you. That's what our God teaches us to do. Forgive your enemies.'

'Forgive your enemies?' Virago muttered. 'Forgive Maggie McKilt?'

'Why not? You have a lot in common … you both hate the Romans, for a start.'

'Forgive your enemies,' Bella said. 'He might have a point.'

Arturo came out waving the book. 'Here it is. The true story of Teutoburger Wald …' he said and sat on the step and began to read it.

***

'The first Roman Emperor, Augustus, conquered Germany, as you know. There was one tribe there called the Cherusci. The Romans were sure the Cherusci loved them…'

'Hah!' Virago snorted. 'The Romans always think that.'

'Well,' Arturo went on, 'the Cherusci had a chief called Arminius and he was so friendly you wouldn't believe it. He went to see the Roman General, Varus, one night … and said there were rebels on the other side of the forest. They were a danger to the Cherusci. They needed the mighty Roman Army to defeat them.'

'A bit like the Picts are rebels on the other side of the Wall?' Bella asked.

'The same,' Arturo nodded. 'Varus said he would lead a legion to crush the rebels … but he didn't know the

125

way. His dear friend, Arminius, offered to show the Roman Army the paths through the horrible gloomy forest they called the Teutoburger Forest.'

'I can see a trap coming,' Virago nodded.

'It was a trap,' Arturo said.

'I told you so, Bella, didn't I tell you?'

'Yes, Virago.'

Arturo jabbed a finger at the book and read on. 'The Romans didn't expect trouble. They took their wives and children with them. The next morning they set off through the forest with carts full of supplies – food and tents, weapons and so on. It was a narrow trail so they had to march in a single line. They were marching along quite happily when they suddenly realized old Arminius and his men had disappeared. The Romans were lost.'

'Well they would be,' Bella nodded.

'A terrible storm broke. The forest turned dark as night. The path turned to a swamp and the wagons sank into it. Then word came back to Varus from the head of the line ... Arminius had returned and was attacking the Romans. The Cherusci ran from the shadows of the trees and chopped down the soldiers, their families too. They started slicing them open and stringing their guts up in the branches of the trees!'

'Ooooh! I say, that's nasty. I mean, I hate the Romans but I'm not sure if I'd slice them open,' Virago muttered.

'You would slice open that Captain Obnoctius if he hurt a hair of your Dandelion's head,' Bella reminded her.

'I would,' the Queen agreed. 'I would.'

Arturo tapped the book again.

127

'Varus was the nephew of Emperor Augustus. He went out of his mind with grief when he heard about the defeat. He went around his palace in Rome, smacking his head against the walls and crying out, 'Varus, oh, Varus, bring me back my legions!' Of course Varus died along with the rest of the legion.' He looked up. 'He took the Roman way out – he fell on to his own sword rather than be captured by the barbarians. So, you see, the Romans can be beaten.'

Virago jumped to her feet and paced the grass. 'We need a rebel tribe ... and we need a swamp,' she said.

'And we need to love our enemies,' Adrian the monk croaked from his cross.

'Which enemies?' Virago asked. 'The Picts or the Romans?'

'The Picts,' Bella said. 'They're just like us in a lot of ways. They've lost their husbands to the Romans. The Romans want to crush them. I think we should love the Picts.'

'The swamp?'

'On the other side of the Wall,' Arturo said.

Virago jumped. 'Wait a moment,' she said. 'Whose side are you on? You're a Roman!'

'I'm a Gaul. Anyway, that Obnoctius shot my best friend over the Wall,' Arturo explained.

Adrian called from his painful perch, 'I say, Virago, you could send Arturo over to the Pict camp to make the peace ... a sort of go-between. The runaway Romans will trust him ... and the Pict Queen will trust him a bit more than you.'

'Adrian, you are brilliant!' Virago said.

'I am even more brilliant when my feet are on the ground and my arms aren't aching fit to drop off,' he moaned. 'Would you like to cut me down?'

Virago sighed. 'The Captain will kill Dandelion if I do.'

Adrian nodded, which hurt because his head clunked against the pole. 'Yes, rescuing your daughter will have to be part of the plan ... and I know just the man to do it... In fact it will fit perfectly! Cut me down and I'll explain.'

Cutting Adrian down was as tricky as putting him up. Arturo climbed on to the Wall and reached over to the leather bands on Adrian's wrists. He chopped and the old monk's hands came free. He fell forward.

Sadly his ankles were still tied so he didn't fall into Virago's waiting arms. He fell face-first into the lower half of the stake. Virago was just tall enough to reach up and slice through the ankle ties which allowed the monk to drop on to the turf on his head.

'Are you all right?' Bella asked and cradled his head in her lap.

'It's better than hanging about all night and day on a pole,' he said. 'But I did get a good view from up there.'

'What did you see?'

'Storm clouds heading this way.'

'Just like Teutoburger Forest?' Virago said. 'It's a sign!'

'It's a sign I should get in the shelter of your hut,' he said and staggered to his feet.

As they hurried over the mound to the village the first huge splashes of rain fell and thunder rumbled over the hills of Britannia.

The evening dark came quickly then was lit with brilliant blue flashes of lightning.

There was one strike that was louder and closer than all the rest. The little group stopped at the door of Virago's hut and looked back. The lightning hit the stake. It lay ruined and smoking against the Wall.

'That could have hurt a bit if you'd still been there.' Virago laughed.

'It's a sign,' Adrian said. 'It's a sign that my plan will work.'

'A sign from the gods?' Bella asked.

'Which gods?' Arturo asked.

'Who cares,' Adrian shrugged. 'Somebody, somewhere, is looking after us. We are going to win!'

TRICKS, TRUMPETS AND TRAPS

A song rose from the bathhouse at the Roman fort on the Wall.

A ROMAN FOR ME, A ROMAN FOR ME
IF YOU'RE NOT A ROMAN YOU'RE NO GOOD TO ME
A GAUL IS A SLAVE
THAT WE WORK TO THE GRAVE
BUT THEY'RE SCARED OF THE ROMANS AND
DON'T MISBEHAVE

'Slave!' Obnoctius called as he stepped from the bath into the steamy air of the hot room. The hot air warmed the floor and he lay on the bench.

A servant hurried in with a jar of scented oil. First he

rubbed the oil into Obnoctius's flabby little body and then he began to scrape the oil off with a flat blade. As he scraped he dragged off the dirt of the day.

'That's right … get rid of the smell of the old monk's vomit,' Obnoctius sighed. 'Nothing like a bath at the end of a good day's work. I taught the Britons and the Picts how we Romans enjoy our games and our feasts. Then I captured one of those Christian cannibal chaps. When he's dead I'll leave him at the Milecastle till the crows have pecked away his eyes and flesh. It'll be a little lesson to the tribes, I think. Of course I'll be in Rome by then … getting my wreath of laurel.'

The Captain closed his eyes. He heard a small cough and looked up. Arturo stood in front of him with a small wooden board. On one side of the board was a thin layer of clay with some words scratched on. 'Sorry, sir,' Arturo said. 'I know you hate to break the rules of the Roman Army. And we aren't really allowed to crucify the old man without a warrant.'

'A warrant?'

'Signed by you, sir. To save you getting into trouble, sir.' Arturo smiled. 'It just says 'I Obnoctius condemn this monk Adrian to death'. If you'd sign the bottom…' Arturo held out the board.

Obnoctius snatched the wooden pens and scratched his name in the soft clay. 'Now get back to the Milecastle and guard the gate. We have to protect our friend Virago.'

'Yes, sir,' Arturo said, bowing as he backed out of the door. He wiped the sweat out of his eyes and looked at the clay tablet. He gently ran a thumb over the words that gave the order for the old man's death. He used the pen to scratch in some new words. 'Free the girl.'

You see? You never know when being able to read and write can come in handy. Maybe you should get someone to teach YOU some day.

Arturo trotted across to the guardhouse and waved the tablet under the Spanish guard's nose. 'Obnoctius wants the girl set free,' he said.

'Aw, he's only just put her in here. She's a load of trouble. Never stopped cursing us. Said she'll do horrible things to us once her mother gets an army together.'

'Maybe that's why the Captain wants to let her go. Maybe he's scared of Virago!'

'Probably,' the Spaniard nodded. He glanced at the clay tablet and said, 'Are you taking her now?'

'Yes,' Arturo said and waited while the Spaniard unlocked the door to the small cell.

Dandelion looked around the door. 'I'm free to go?'

She saw Arturo standing there. 'You've come to take me home?'

'Yes ... but hurry before ... before your mother starts a war! She's upset,' Arturo said quickly.

'Upset? She'll probably fight that little Roman with one hand behind her back ... two hands behind her back.'

Dandelion sniffed. 'She'd bite him to death. Let's go!'

The two made their way up onto the Wall and walked past some dozing guards. The storm had blown over now leaving puddles shining silver in the light of a half moon. They passed the first milecastle and the guards saw Arturo's uniform and waved him through.

Arturo's milecastle was deserted. They hurried down the steps, over the muddy grass and the slippery mound to Queen Virago's hut.

The British Queen wrapped her arms around her daughter and crushed her in a massive hug. The monk Adrian smiled and said. 'Part one complete. Off you go, Arturo. Part two. The tricky part…'

***

Don was the first Pict out of bed at sunrise. He climbed the hill by the village and looked across to the Milecastle. Maybe he could climb the Wall and look for his ball before the Britons started stirring. Maybe that British girl would … no, that was a stupid idea. Ball-foot wasn't for girls.

In the faint morning light he saw the Milecastle gate open. A Roman soldier came out and headed straight towards him. When the soldier looked up and saw Don he waved in a friendly way and strode across the marshy ground.

'No!' Don called. 'There was a storm last night. The swamp's too deep to cross … you'll not make it. You'll have to go round!'

The soldier nodded and walked to the drier paths to the west then came round to the Pictish village. 'It's the foot-ball boy,' he said.

'It's ball-foot. And you're the man that fires people out of catapults!' Don said fiercely.

Arturo spread his hands. 'I was only doing what I was told. That was my best friend I killed,' he added. 'Don't think I enjoyed it.'

'You didn't kill him,' Don said. 'We saved him. He's joined us.'

Arturo's face showed great relief. 'Great news!' he cried. 'I think there are a few more would like to join you,' Arturo said. 'Let me talk to your Queen Maggie and see if we can come up with a plan to set us all free. You'd like to be free, wouldn't you?'

Don scratched his head. 'Does this plan include me getting my football back?'

'I think we can manage that,' Arturo nodded.

'Then follow me ... and I'll tell the tribe not to kill you.'

'Love your enemy,' Arturo said brightly.

'You're soft in the head,' the boy jeered. 'If we love our enemies then who do we get to fight?'

'The Romans,' Arturo grinned. 'The Romans.'

***

Obnoctius marched out. 'Parp-parp-a-parp-parp.' The troop of a hundred men scared every bird for miles around. The fort had been emptied. Everyone was ordered to join the search.

'The girl escaped!' the Captain raged as he jabbed the guard with his spear and made him march along the Wall at the head of the Spanish troop. 'You let her escape!'

'I had your order, sir ... your signature on the tablet!'

'It was a trick … you idiot … you were tricked!' Jab-jab.

'Ouch, sir … I thought you were the one that was tricked.'

Jab-jab, 'Don't argue, Spanish fool. You let a dangerous prisoner go free.'

'Dangerous?'

'A hostage. Without her Virago could do anything – even set that monk free,' Obnoctius cried and jabbed harder.

When he reached Milecastle 13 he stopped and looked at the burnt, split stake. It was empty. 'See! See? What did I tell you? You can take the monk's place on the stake you simple-minded soldier. You and that Arturo who was supposed to stay on guard. You can be tied to the stake together.'

'Won't it be a bit crowded, sir?'

'I don't care!' the captain screamed and stamped his foot, '… so long as you suffer for this disaster. I don't care, see?' Obnoctius spluttered.

'But, sir, Virago and the Brigantes haven't taken the girl and run away … look. They're still in their village,' the soldier said.

'Virago!' Obnoctius called. 'Come here you evil woman.'

'Virago and the women and children ran over the mound and as Obnoctius reached the bottom of the tower steps they threw themselves at his feet, wailing. 'Oh, Captain, our Captain. Save us, Captain. Our hero!'

'Hero!' the villagers cried.

Obnoctius was confused … as he was supposed to be. That was the plan.

'Where is Adrian the Monk?' Obnoctius demanded. 'He was here when I left last night. Who cut him down?

They will suffer for it – they will take his place … along with the guard who released your daughter and Arturo who should have been keeping watch. They will all be killed together!'

'Won't it be a bit crowded?' Virago asked.

'Stop saying that,' the little Roman ranted. 'Answer the question … where has he gone?'

'Oh, Captain, sir, hero … we fear he's been stolen.'

'Stolen? Who would want to steal a smelly old man who looks like a badly dressed goat?'

'The Attacotti, sir,' Virago moaned.

'The cannibals? Are they in the area?' Obnoctius blinked.

'We think so, sir,' Bella put in with a sad sniffle. 'We think they climbed the Wall in the night and snatched your guard, Arturo, as he brought my daughter back from the fort. Then they stole the old man … for afters.'

'They stole them to … to eat them?' Obnoctius asked.

'That's what we think,' Virago said and the Britons nodded.

'Won't he be a bit tough to eat? A bit old and stringy?'

Virago shrugged. 'Sorry, sir … I wouldn't know. I've never eaten an old man. Maybe you have…'

'Don't be ridiculous, woman. I'm a Roman. We don't eat people! We're not that wicked.'

'No, sir,' the British Queen sighed. 'You don't eat people. You let lions and crocodiles eat them. You let bulls gore them with their sharp horns and bears rip their flesh off with their cruel claws. You burn them alive. You turn them into slaves and drag them over the roads of Rome with hooks through their flesh. You kill criminals in your games for fun and you send Spanish men to shiver on the Wall while our husbands are torn from us and sent to melt in the desert suns. But you don't eat people. It's good to know you're not that wicked.'

'True,' Obnoctius smirked.

'So I hope you will help the poor Queen to rescue her friend Adrian and her daughter Dandelion ... sir.'

'They will be long gone by now.' Obnoctius sighed. 'Into the hills of Pictland.'

'No,' Bella said. 'They will be in the Pict village over the hill. We can see the smoke from their fires. If we can get to them before dinner time we may save the victims from being the dinner!'

Obnoctius nodded. 'It's worth a try,' he said. The Captain began to order the Spanish troops into a line at the Milecastle gate. Obnoctius himself stood at the front and made a little speech. 'Friends, Romans, countrymen ... pay attention, that man at the back. We are going to invade Pictland and show these Britons why they are better off under the rule of Rome. We will rescue their friends and family. We will destroy their foul foes and make the Wall a safe place for children to play and women to weave. We will march to death or glory!'

The Spanish troop nodded gloomily. Obnoctius coughed. 'I think three cheers for my speech would be a good idea.'

'Can we get moving, sir? It's a bit cold,' one of the men muttered.

'To the gates and glory!' Obnoctius cried. 'Trumpeter

… sound the attack!'

'Sorry sir, I sat on me trumpet,' the man said.

Obnoctius glared at him as he led his hundred warriors in silence into the land of the enemy. The British women gathered stones from the Pictish side of the Wall and hurried to stack them beside the catapult. The troops marched forward.

***

A small figure stood in the middle of the marsh between the troop and the Pictish village. The Captain squinted at him. It was that boy again. 'Stop!' the boy cried. He was two hundred paces from the troop but they could hear him. The men clattered to a ragged halt.

'Speak, boy!' Obnoctius called to him.

'The marsh is soft. See where I am standing? It is firm ground. Walk straight towards me and you will be safe.' Obnoctius turned to the troop. 'Walk straight towards that British boy, men. He is our guide.'

'Haven't you heard the tale of Varus in the Teutoburger Wald?' a soldier asked him,

'I am not Varus and this is not Teutoburger,' Obnoctius laughed. 'I am not a fool. I know a trap when I see one. The boy is standing on firm ground. What more do you need to see? Forward, men!'

'Hurry!' Don cried. 'Hurry or you'll be too late!'

And they marched forward.

At first the mud oozed over their sandals. The men struggled to pull their feet out of the oozing slime. Soon they were knee deep in the swamp and unable to move.

'Keep going men,' Obnoctius cried. 'See? The boy is on firm ground.'

But no one moved – except Don McKilt. He raised one foot from the place where he stood and the soldiers could see it was fastened to a wooden pole. 'Stilts,' Don laughed as he stepped carefully back from the swamp and towards the hill by the village.

He took off the stilts and ran up the hill. He called down the other side, 'The flies are in the spider's web, Ma!'

The Picts along with the warriors, Dandelion, Arturo, Walli and Adrian came to the top of the hill and looked down. 'Surrender, Obnoctius. Surrender or die.'

'A Roman chooses to die!' he called back. 'We will never surrender. We will fight you on the beaches, we will fight you in the deserts, we will fight you in sticky, horrible, cold, Pictish swamps ... but we will never surrender!'

ENDINGS

Don McKilt put two fingers into his mouth and blew a sharp whistle. The Picts made a roof from their shields — what the Romans called a tortoise — because they knew what was coming next.

> When I say Picts, you will remember they are actually Gaul deserters who used to fight for Rome. Just checking in case you were wondering why Picts would fight in the Roman style.

There was a whoosh as a catapult load of stones rained down on the Roman soldiers, trapped in the sticky ooze.

The men cried out but Obnoctius just yelled, 'No surrender!'

Don whistled and more stones fell. A Spanish soldier pulled the battered helmet off his head. 'We surrender!'

'We don't!' Obnoctius objected.

'We surrender ... he doesn't,' the Spaniard said wearily. 'Now get us out of here before we drown.'

The warriors ran to the edge of the swamp and threw ropes to the soldiers who stood, dripping slime and shivering.

You're a disgrace to the Roman Army!' Obnoctius screamed.

'We're not in the Roman Army any longer,' one of the

legion laughed. 'We resign.' The others cheered and the men tramped over the hill to the village to find new, dry clothes.

'What about me?' the Captain wailed.

'You said you wanted to die,' Dandelion reminded him.

'Ah, yes … no … no … I want to die as a true Roman – I want to fall on my sword like Varus did.'

'Isn't that a bit messy?' Don asked. 'You'll get blood all over your lovely uniform – probably turn your armour rusty too.'

Obnoctius struggled to pull the short sword from his belt but he was already sunk to the waist. At last he tugged it free and placed it against his stomach.

'Aren't you supposed to put the sharp end to your belly, not the handle?' Don asked.

'I don't know,' the Captain frowned. 'I haven't done this before. I'll try it this way first. He clutched the handle to his belly button and leaned forward. The sword vanished into the swamp.

'Oh, dear.' Don laughed. 'How can you fall on your sword when your sword's at the bottom of a swamp. There must be other ways of killing a Roman.'

'Well, sometimes we sting victims to death with nettles … and sometimes we throw them off a high cliff in Rome – the Tarpeian Rock.'

'There you are! Throw yourself off the top of Milecastle 13,' Don said. He threw a rope across to the Captain and the man hauled himself out of the mud. The Captain lay panting on the edge of the swamp for a while, getting his breath back.

The Picts and the Spanish soldiers who had deserted

their army marched past him. They waved goodbye to the British and Pict women who stood arm in arm on the hill top. The old monk, Adrian, shuffled along beside them.

'Are you going home?' Don asked.

'Yes,' Walli told him. 'We'll march down to the River Tyne and see if we can find a trading boat to take us to Gaul and Spain.'

'You could stay,' Don said. 'Ma will miss you.'

'I know,' Walli said. 'But it's just too cold and wild up here ... especially for the poor Spanish. They want to get back to the sun before the Pictish wind kills them.'

Don sighed. 'I'll come through the gate with you ... see if I can find my football.'

Dandelion ran down the hill and joined him at the head of the line. 'Isn't it boring, kicking a ball against a wall?' she asked.

'I kick it into a coal,' the boy said and he explained the rules.

'But it would be better if I tried to kick it into your coal and you tried to kick it into mine. The one who scores the most coals is the winner!' she said.

Don frowned and thought about it. 'Could some of the lads from my village help me?'

'Yes,' Dandelion nodded. 'If I can have some of the girls from my village helping me. We would attack you with the foot-ball just like our fathers used to attack one another with spears and swords.'

Don nodded. 'Britannia against Pictland? It could be exciting ... war without killing.'

And the two young enemies were so busy chatting they

passed through the gates, passed the catapult and climbed the mound without noticing what was waiting for them on the other side.

By then it was too late.

A Roman general sat on a white horse, his helmet plumes streaming in the wind. Beside him a soldier carried a tall pole with a carved Roman eagle on the top. The standard bearer.

They looked powerful and scary, even to tough fighters like Dandelion and Don. But worse. A massed legion of armed soldiers stood in rows behind them. There must have been a thousand, Dandelion guessed. She turned to shout a warning to the men.

By chance Captain Obnoctius had been the last through the Milecastle gates. He had closed and barred it behind him. After all, it was his job.

They were trapped.

The general looked down. 'Are you Picts or British?' he asked.

'We're Gauls and Spanish in the Roman Army,' Walli said.

Arturo jumped forward. 'We've just been raiding in Pictland – we disguised ourselves as natives and we slaughtered about a hundred!'

Did we?' Walli asked.

'Maybe two hundred.'

'Where is your Captain?' the general asked.

Obnoctius stepped forward. He looked at the ground in shame – his legs were muddied, his helmet and armour bent and beaten with stones. 'Well done, Captain,' the general said. 'There could be a laurel wreath waiting for you in Rome – a small army like this defeating two hundred barbarians!'

Obnoctius looked bright. 'That man is a Gaul – he never learned to count. It was probably about five hundred, sir.'

'Amazing. And I see you have found the man we are searching for ... that looks like the monk, Adrian.'

'Yes, sir, we captured the cannibal ... maybe you'd like to see him killed?'

'Again?' Adrian squawked. 'Once is enough for any man.'

'Hah!' the general snorted. 'Killed? No, man. Saint Adrian is a hero of the Roman Empire.'

'He is?' Obnoctius gasped.

'I am?' Adrian said faintly.

'Yes … you met the Emperor's mother, Helena, and preached to her,' the general reminded him.

'Then I had to flee for my life.' Adrian nodded.

'Ah, but Emperor Constantine defeated his enemy Maxentius and his mother said it was down to your Christian God. Constantine became a Christian and the orders are the whole Roman Empire will become Christian. Love your enemies, Captain!'

'Love my enemies?'

'Yes, that's the new Roman way. Get your men back to the fort, get them smartened up … they're going home. And you can escort Adrian back to Rome – the Emperor will probably want to honour you both! This new army from Tungria will take over your guard duties.'

Obnoctius pulled his shoulders back and stuck out his chest … except it didn't stick out quite as much as his tubby stomach. 'Right, troop, you heard the general. Into line and quick march!'

The deserters looked at the tough Tungrians and decided it wasn't the time to get into a fight. Not if they were going home anyway.

Walli and Arturo said a quick 'goodbye' to Don and Dandelion and shambled after Obnoctius.

'The village is deserted,' the general said.

'Yes, the British are all over the Wall making friends with the Picts … the way Adrian told us to,' Don explained.

'Splendid,' the general said. 'One day we may be able to do without the Wall. One day Britannia and Pictland will be one.'

Of course Britannia and Pictland became England and Scotland. England and Scotland DID become one ... sort of. But there are still a lot of England-scorning Scots to the north of the border and haggis-hating English to the south. Some things never change.

He led his massive army east towards the fort and left the two children bewildered and wondering.

Don picked up his ball. 'No Wall?'

'Brits and Picts all the same country? Who would we play football against then? The Romans? The Spanish?'

'Nah. Ball-foot's a game for tough, northern lads ... if that lot can't stand the cold they'll never make ball-footers.'

'And northern girls,' Dandelion insisted.

'And northern girls.' Don sighed. He picked up his pig's bladder and let it bounce off his head.

'The Romans rule the world today ... but one day the British will rule the world with football,' she crowed.

'The Scots will always be better,' Don sniffed.

'In your dreams,' Dandelion jeered. 'You really think the Romans will lose their power one day soon?' Dandelion asked.

'One day when the Wall falls down and Pictland is free,' Don said. 'So we'd better start practising now.'

He kicked the ball towards the Wall and ran after it. Soon the cries of Dandelion and Don playing were heard across the Wall and they opened the gates to let the others through. Soon there were eleven on each side and Don said, 'That's enough. It's just right. Ball-foot will always be played with eleven on each side.'

'But it will always be war without swords,' Dandelion said and kicked his shin before racing past him with the bladder and lashing it into the coal. 'Here we go! Here we go! Here we go!' she cried as the British girls threw their arms around her and kissed her.

'Girls,' Don spat. 'You won't get boys kissing each other over a silly coal.'

But when the Romans, the Gauls and the Spanish had left – and when the Picts and British women came to watch the game – the Wall looked down on twenty-two excited players. When Don scored a coal his team kissed him and he didn't seem to mind. 'Picts one, Brits one!' Queen Virago and Queen Maggie McKilt cheered.

They played on till it was too dark to see the ball in the shadow of the great old Wall. Two weary but happy tribes went back to their villages with a vow to meet again on the battlefield.

'You know, Maggie,' Virago said '…you don't mind me calling you Maggie?'

'Not at all, Vira.'

You know, Maggie, I think we may have started something. We could play this football game every week in the winter – until it gets too hot over the summer.'

'Nah … you'll soon get tired of getting beaten,' Maggie laughed.

'I think not,' Virago said, suddenly stiff as a hedgehog's bristle.

'I think so…'

'Not!'

'So!'

'Not!'

'So!'

Their screeching voices were drowned by the cries of the night owls and the howl of the Pictish winds.

And the war went on with a pig bladder in place of a sword. And it probably always will.

EPILOGUE

Here's an odd thing … Hadrian's Wall is one of the greatest marvels of the ancient world. It was so great you can still see large parts of it now, 1,900 years after it was built.

Yet no one is sure what it was for.

Different people will tell you different stories. It is said the Roman Wall was:

• To keep the Picts out – like a fortress wall
• To keep the British in – like a prison wall
• To collect taxes from traders – like a customs barrier
• To mark the end of the Roman Empire – like a garden wall

We will never know. But we can get a bit of a 'feel' for the Wall. The men of Rome wouldn't visit too often. But imagine what it must have been like for the men of Gaul or Spain or anywhere in the south of the massive Roman Empire. Men used to the sun went to the Wall and felt the chill of a Pictish wind. Those Wall guards must have suffered … and grumbled.

At last they gave it up. The warriors of the world – the men the Romans called 'Barbarians' – ganged up on Rome and fought back. In AD 406 the Germans – the terrors of Teutoburger – crossed the River Rhine into the Empire. By 410 they were at the gates of Rome. The ancient city was smashed by an enemy force for the first time in almost 800 years.

The Cherusci had beaten the Romans terribly in Teutoburger ... now their great-great (actually quite a few greats) grandchildren finished the job.

Romans fought on for another 60 years but really it was all over for the Roman Empire.

Places like the Colosseum in Rome were where Christians and criminals, bears and boars, all sorts of birds and beasts had died horribly. Now it's a crumbling ruin.

Even the Wall is small since farmers have stolen the stones to build their barns. Now the stones that are left look down on the grey ghosts and the terrible tourists.

THIS IS SO BORING CAN'T WE JUST PLAY FOOTBALL?

If you enjoyed Wall of Woe, then you'll love three more Gory Stories, written by Terry Deary. Why not read the whole horrible lot?

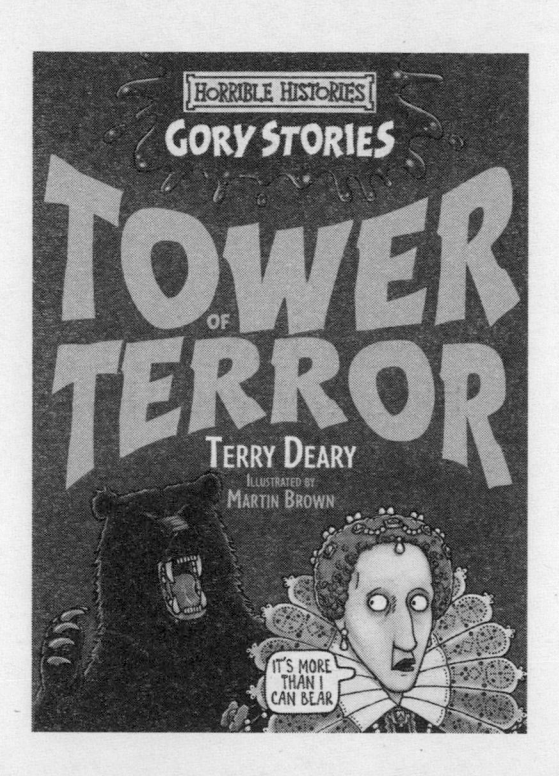

S imon Tuttle and his Pa are tricksters struggling to make a living on the Tudor streets. When disaster strikes Simon must fend for himself, even if it means committing treason. But can he pull off his Pa's carefully concocted plan and should he trust his mysterious new accomplice?

Find out in this Terrible Tudor adventure, it's got all the gore and so much more!

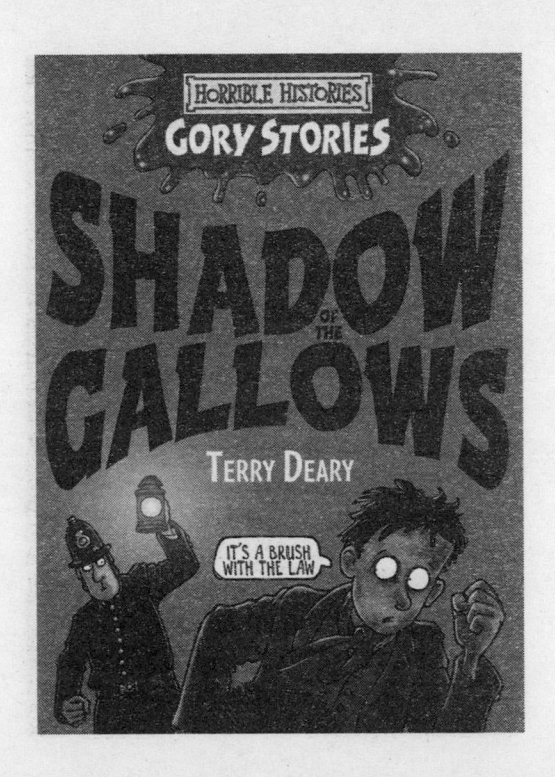

When a boy called Bairn is rescued from his dangerous job as an Edinburgh chimney sweep, he appears to have landed on his feet. But his new job proves just as dangerous and he soon becomes caught up in a plot to kill Queen Victoria. Has he been saved from slavery only to end up swinging at the gallows?

Find out in this Vile Victorian adventure, it's got all the gore and so much more!

Phoul Pharaoh Tutankhamun has died and is about to be buried. It's master-thief Antef's big moment – can he and his crew of criminals pull off the biggest grave-robbery of all time and empty Tut's tomb of its richest treasures?

Find out in this Awful Egyptian adventure,
it's got all the gore and so much more!

Don't miss these horribly handy Handbooks for all the gore and more!

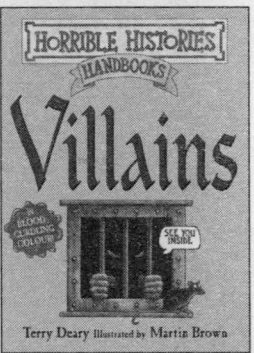

Terry Deary was born at a very early age, so long ago he can't remember. But his mother, who was there at the time, says he was born in Sunderland, north-east England, in 1946 – so it's not true that he writes all *Horrible Histories* from memory. At school he was a horrible child only interested in playing football and giving teachers a hard time. His history lessons were so boring and so badly taught, that he learned to loathe the subject. *Horrible Histories* is his revenge.

Martin Brown was born in Melbourne, on the proper side of the world. Ever since he can remember he's been drawing. His dad used to bring back huge sheets of paper from work and Martin would fill them with doodles and little figures. Then, quite suddenly, with food and water, he grew up, moved to the UK and found work doing what he's always wanted to do: drawing doodles and little figures.